FERAL NATION

Infiltration

ALSO BY SCOTT B. WILLIAMS

The Pulse
Refuge
Voyage After the Collapse
Landfall
Horizons
Enter the Darkness
The Darkness After
Into the River Lands
The Forge of Darkness
The Savage Darkness
Sailing the Apocalypse
On Island Time: Kayaking the Caribbean

ISBN-13: 978-1976219399
Cover photographs: Fotolia # 140148371 © Getmilitaryphotos, Fotolia #100579897 © Stephan Orsillo
Cover & interior design: Scott B. Williams
Editors: Michelle Cleveland, Bill Barker

FERAL NATION
Infiltration

Scott B. Williams
Feral Nation Series Book One

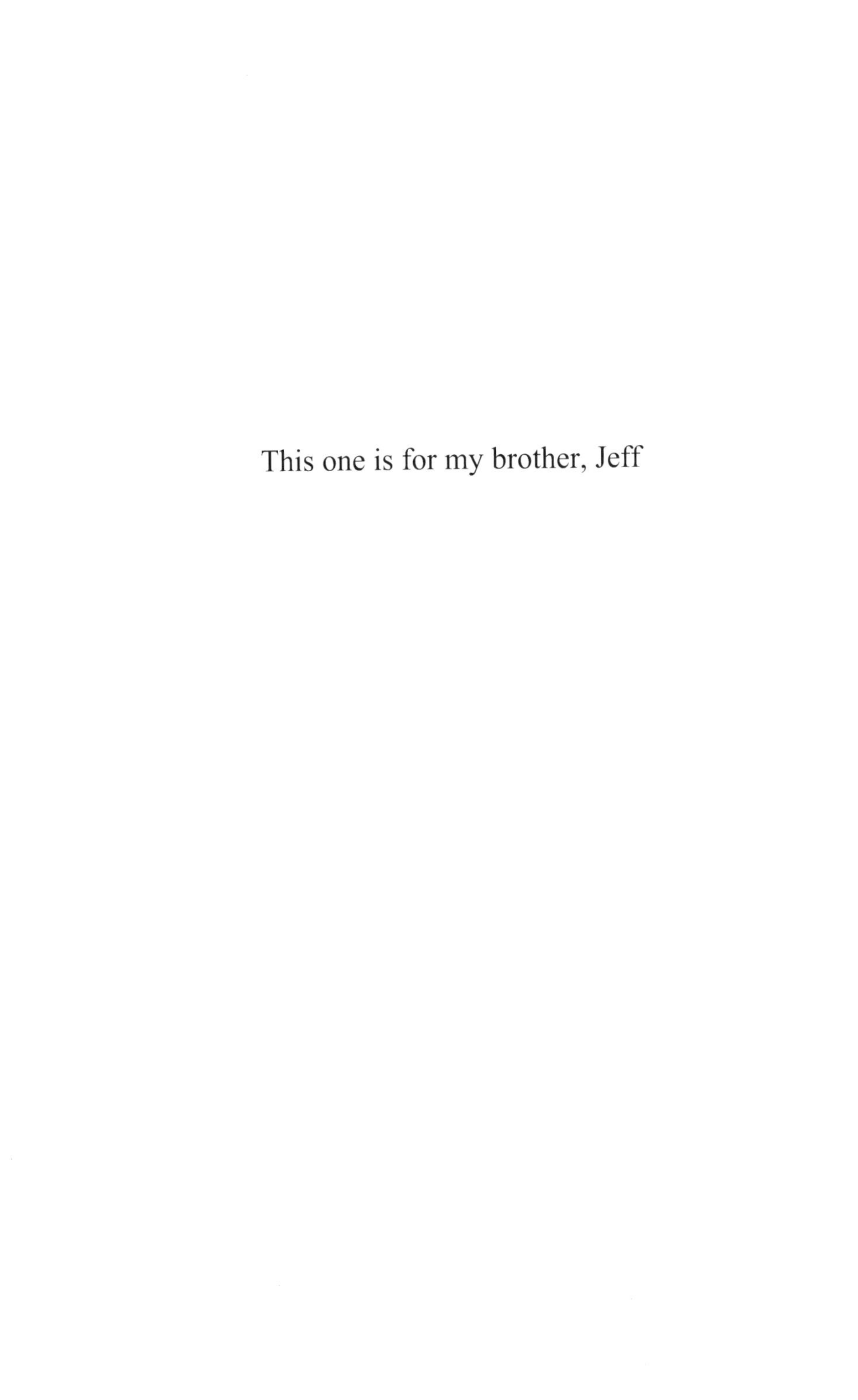

This one is for my brother, Jeff

One

Eric Branson paused to study the dark outline of land a half mile ahead of him, resting his double-ended paddle across the coaming of the cockpit as he let the kayak drift for a moment on the rain-spattered swells. He could hear the sound of moderate surf breaking in the distance, crashing onto the jetties and the public beach on the south side of Jupiter Inlet. Eric knew the layout of the city park on that side from many lazy Sunday afternoons spent there years ago with Shauna and Megan. Even back then the park side of the inlet would have been mostly dark and deserted this time of morning, as it was still almost two hours until daybreak. But back then, the condominiums farther south and the houses, restaurants and marinas along the shore inside of the cut would have been brightly lit. Now the entire coast was dark, just as Eric had expected, but darkness was his ally now and he was grateful for the concealment it provided.

He scanned the shoreline with his night vision monocular as he sat there drifting, looking for movement or other indications of activity on either side of the entrance. The waterproof handheld VHF radio secured to the deck in front of him remained silent, despite the digital scanner function he'd set to monitor all the major marine frequencies. No one was talking on the airwaves, but he turned the volume down anyway, as he would soon be within earshot of the shore. He had stopped paddling just beyond the first of the channel markers that led the way to the inlet from the open Atlantic, to watch and listen before the final approach. A few of the flashing red and green lights were still working, running off their self-contained solar charged batteries, but others were misplaced or missing entirely, no doubt swept away by the storm surge from the recent hurricane.

Eric didn't need to stay in the channel to safely transit the narrow cut in his kayak, but doing so would keep him as far as possible from the jetties on either side. He wasn't worried about hitting the rocks but he *was* concerned that someone could be out there, hidden from view among the shadows. The blackout ashore and the light rain that limited visibility would provide the concealment he needed, but any covert insertion on a hostile coast entailed risk. Going solo and without backup increased that risk exponentially, but that was nothing new to Eric. What *was* new was that he was doing something of this nature here—on the east coast of Florida—a place he'd once called home.

The oil tanker that he'd worked his Atlantic passage aboard as part of the security team had long since disappeared unlit into the night. Eric had disembarked five miles off the coast at the edge of the Gulf Stream current, just as he had prearranged with the captain before departing Tenerife. It had taken him more than an hour and a half to close on the coast from the drop point, paddling at a steady, but moderate pace to stay fresh for whatever he might encounter at landfall. The 17-foot, matte black Klepper folding kayak was seaworthy and capable of hauling a lot of gear, but it certainly wasn't a swift boat, especially with a solo paddler. Eric was alone here tonight because he wasn't part of a team on a mission to take out a specific target or recon for a bigger operation. It was personal business that brought him back to the U.S. mainland because he could no longer ignore all that he'd heard, as unimaginable as it seemed from afar. The only people in the world that had ever really cared about him were somewhere beyond that dark shoreline ahead... *if* they were still alive. Eric had failed them both in the past, especially Shauna, his former wife who had since moved on to someone new, and Megan, his only child who grew up with a father that was gone more often than not. Eric couldn't change the past, but he thought perhaps he could make up for some of his failings now. Maybe now the skills at which he excelled would finally be of use to them.

The *Aquila Mia* was bound for Veracruz, so the course deviation en route to the Straits of Florida was relatively minor. Eric chose this point of insertion not only because he was familiar with the coast and the Intracoastal Waterway here, but also because it was close to his first and most important destination. Entering the country legally at any official point of entry, if there was one even open now, was not an option with the gear he had in the kayak. Getting it in this way was worth the risk because Eric was sure he was going to need it if things here were indeed as bad as the rumors.

Infiltrating this coast undetected would have been more difficult in normal circumstances. The authorities in Florida had spent decades perfecting their drug interdiction techniques and after 9/11 Homeland Security tightened the net even further. But illicit cargo and illegal aliens still got through from time to time even then, and based on what he'd heard of the situation now, Eric was willing to take the gamble. The simple truth was that a lone 17-foot kayak approaching from the open ocean on a dark and rainy night was unlikely to be noticed. Such a craft was too small and too lacking in reflective materials to generate a radar signature, and this particular inlet wasn't near any sensitive military or civilian targets with sophisticated surveillance anyway. Now that a major hurricane had finished the job of breaking down the infrastructure, Eric was more concerned about being spotted by a vigilante property owner with a rifle than he was about arrest or interdiction by the authorities. If the reports he'd heard were true, any remaining law enforcement officers that hadn't abandoned their duties in the interests of self-preservation would have their hands full enough. But Eric had to consider that some random civilian might shoot without hesitation if he was seen sneaking across the water at this hour. He would be within easy rifle range of the shore while traversing the inlet and for much of the rest of his route, but he was counting on the cloak of rain and the stealth of the kayak to avoid becoming a target.

The tide was rising as he entered the cut; a good thing because Jupiter Inlet was notorious in wind against tide conditions. Eric remembered when he lived here before that all too often there was a local news story of someone capsizing a sizable boat in the breakers there. The Klepper could handle rough conditions better than many much larger boats, but Eric had no desire to prove that tonight. He had barely two hours of darkness left and he didn't want to waste them. His first priority was getting inside to sheltered waters, and then finding a place to hole up and study his route until nightfall came again. The satellite images and offline maps he'd downloaded onto his smartphone before he'd left Europe were all he had to go on to locate his primary objective. He still had his handheld Garmin GPS receiver, but like the GPS receivers aboard the *Aquila Mia*, it was unable to lock on a sufficient number of satellites to get a fix. It was obvious that the signals had been turned off or scrambled deliberately, no doubt in the interest of national security.

It didn't matter now because Eric didn't need GPS accuracy for this mission anyway. He'd made the open water crossing after leaving the ship by compass bearing alone, and the rest of the route would be inshore. Once he was through the cut all he had to do was turn south onto the Intracoastal Waterway and keep paddling until he found a place to lie low. His drop off had been later in the night than he'd hoped, so there wasn't enough time to get where he was going before dawn. It was inconvenient, but he had to accept that it would take part of a second night of travel to get there and that keeping a low profile was more important than speed at this point anyway. Eric had never been to the upscale waterfront neighborhood where Shauna and Megan had lived since the divorce, so he would be relying on his stored images to find the correct house. Shauna's new husband hadn't wanted him coming there at all and Eric hadn't pressed the issue. The last time he'd seen his daughter, Shauna and Megan met him at his father's place near LaBelle, and Eric had been fine with that. He had no interest in Daniel Hartfield or the lavish lifestyle the man provided his ex. He was good to Megan, and as long as he remained so, Eric had no beef with him. Along with Daniel came his 12-year-old son, Andrew from a previous marriage, and apparently the four of them got along just fine.

Although Shauna had been living it up as the wife and stepmother of her new family, it wasn't like she and Megan were doing without before. Even when Eric was still on Uncle Sam's payroll his salary and benefits had been sufficient to provide for them. When he took up private contracting after his last team mission in Afghanistan, the money was far better and the bulk of it went straight home to his wife and daughter. Money, or the lack thereof, wasn't the problem. The real problem was that Shauna wanted Eric *home.* But although he tried more than once to make that happen, Eric couldn't readjust to civilian life after all he'd seen and done. He was a professional warrior because it was what he was born to be, and it was the one thing he was exceptionally good at. Nothing in civilian life could compare to the intricate planning and execution of small-team Special Ops missions, or the high-risk contracts he'd been offered since. The turmoil of the post 9/11 world provided ample opportunity to pursue his destiny, and a life without danger and adventure seemed like no life at all to Eric Branson.

As the terrorism and mayhem heated up around the globe, Eric's opportunities as a security contractor were virtually limitless. He'd worked all over the Middle East and parts of Asia and Africa in the early days, and more recently in several countries in Europe. There was no end in sight to the demand for his skills, but none of those opportunities were compatible with family life. He came back to visit when he could, but somehow the years slipped by and before he knew it, Eric was divorced and his little girl was in college.

The last time he'd seen Megan, a few months after missing her high school graduation, she seemed more distant than ever. She wasn't proud of the work her father did and Eric knew she might never understand why it was necessary. Would the events that had transpired in the past several months have made a difference in her thinking? Eric didn't know, but he *did* know it was time to come back. His country was coming apart at the seams, and he knew he wouldn't know the full extent of it until he saw it for himself firsthand.

The recent news he'd gotten from overseas was sketchy, but apparently gas shortages, roadblocks and no fly zones had the country locked down and immobile. Power and communication grids in many of the larger cities were disabled or crippled as the government sought to maintain control and crush the riots and uprisings. Everyone was suffering from the resultant shortages of food and other essential goods whether they were directly involved or not. To make matters here in Florida even worse, a major hurricane struck the peninsula near Fort Lauderdale just weeks before, leaving south Florida devastated. Eric had been working off the grid all summer prior to that, and upon learning the news at the conclusion of his mission; he'd been unable to reach Shauna or Megan or his father or brother back in the States. With everything else that was already going on there, Eric knew that it would get ugly in Florida real fast. Hurricane victims were going to be cut off and stranded, with food running out and no help coming from outside the region because of all the other problems.

The only thing left was to come here and find his loved ones and get them out to some place safer. Eric had quickly wrapped up his obligations overseas and found a way to get here as soon as possible. Since flying wasn't an option, he came the best way he knew how, and now that he was here, the effects of the storm's aftermath were clearly evident as he scanned the unlit coast before him. When he put away the monocular and picked up the paddle again, his only fear as he closed the final gap to the jetties was that he might already be too late.

Two

THE RAIN PROVIDED THE concealment he'd hoped for as Eric paddled through the inlet and then past the dark silhouettes of the houses lining the shore to the north. He made his way west past the tall coconut palms of the park, aiming for the middle of the highway bridge that he had to paddle under to reach the ICW channel leading south. He couldn't see or hear any vehicle traffic moving on the bridge, but before getting too close he stopped and scanned it for pedestrians with the monocular. Passing beneath the span put him in a vulnerable position, even from someone armed only with rocks or other objects they might throw down at him. But though he checked carefully, taking his time to be thorough, Eric saw nothing. Even in normal times he would have expected things to be quiet on a rainy night at 0430 hours, but this was a different kind of quiet, and he imagined there was a curfew in effect if there was still any law enforcement operating at all. The well-to-do communities in this part of Palm Beach County had a significant and effective police presence before, but he wondered if they'd managed to hold it together now.

If there were police or military patrols, Eric figured their attention would be focused on the roads, and if so, bridges would be critical points of interest. This one seemed completely abandoned though, increasing Eric's suspicions that things might be worse here than he'd feared.

With the Intracoastal Waterway cutting right through these upscale communities, Eric knew too that there might be surveillance on the waterways. If so, it would likely be targeting larger vessels than his low-profile sea kayak. Eric's experience with waterborne insertions had taught him that unconventional alternatives were often overlooked, so he remained confident that he could evade detection as long as he took it slow and stayed alert.

Once he was under the bridge, he passed a large marina wrapped around the point on his left leading into the southbound ICW. Nothing was moving on any of the docks that he could see, and he heard no generators or other signs of life. There were a few dim lights visible through the portlights of some of the yachts, but Eric didn't know if that meant they were occupied or that the owners had simply left them turned on. Modern LED lighting powered by the large house batteries aboard such vessels could run for a long time unattended, and there was nothing else here to indicate they were otherwise. Some of the motor and sail yachts he could see were clearly damaged by the hurricane, as evidenced by bent bow rails and stanchions and wind-ripped canvas awnings and sails. It was as if the owners hadn't bothered to prepare them to weather the storm, likely because of all the other problems in the area that had already taken their attention away from such trivial things as their personal pleasure craft.

Turning south onto the ICW, Eric found himself in an area where the waterfront homes and businesses were interspersed with designated natural areas and parks. In some of these places, dense tangles of mangroves and sea grapes grew right to the water's edge. Cruising slowly and peering into them, Eric spotted a channel winding among the roots and branches in one such place, ending on a narrow sand bar barely visible from the waterway. He'd been confined to the kayak long enough that he needed to get out and stretch his legs, and with the open water crossing behind him and dawn coming, it was time to find a place to wait out the day. The little strip of beach was hidden from the road that paralleled the waterway farther west, but Eric knew from living here before that some of these nature preserves were laced with hiking trails leading in from the roads. He studied the dark woods beyond the sandbar through the monocular and satisfied that he was alone, paddled to the end of the channel and stepped out in the ankle-deep water, pulling the bow of the boat onto the bar. The first phase of his covert entry had gone spectacularly well and he had successfully landed on American soil unnoticed. After traversing the most dangerous zone between the open ocean and the outer fringe of coast, he was in, and for all anyone who might see him knew, had never left the country at all.

After stretching his arms and legs, Eric reached into the kayak and opened the dry bag he kept in the cockpit to retrieve his water bottle, snacks and smartphone. This was exactly the kind of place he'd been hoping to find. He would have preferred to get closer to Shauna's house, but it was too close to dawn to risk going farther, not knowing if he'd find another hideout as good as this one. As it was, he wouldn't have far to go the following evening, and if all went as planned, he would arrive there well after midnight, when the neighborhood was asleep. Then he would simply sit tight at the dock behind her house until daybreak, as he didn't want to alarm anyone inside. It would be nice if he didn't have to see Daniel Hartfield, but if Shauna and Megan and especially Andrew were there, Eric was sure Daniel would be too. If Megan *was* there, then Eric could rest easy. The only other person he had to worry about in Florida was his father, but he knew Bart Branson could take care of himself as well as anyone, so there was less urgency to reach him right away. Eric imagined they would all need to get out of the region soon, but he would discuss that with Megan and her mom when he found them. There was also the matter of his brother Keith and his wife Lynn. Keith and Lynn lived in rural south Louisiana, a long way from the troubles here in

Florida, but that didn't mean they were necessarily safe. Keith was as dedicated to his job as a law enforcement officer could be though, and things would have to be worse than hopeless for him to walk away from it. Eric would have a better idea of the chances of that after he spent some time assessing the situation here first hand. For now though, he had to focus on one thing at a time.

He stood next to the kayak munching on a handful of almonds as he powered up the phone to study his downloaded images and maps. The device was useless for communications here, but it was still a capable handheld computer with many valuable offline functions. In the kayak he carried a portable battery bank for it as well as a small, flexible solar panel to keep it and his other electronic devices charged. He easily pinpointed his location in the nature park and scrolled the imagery south along the waterway to the canal entrance that led to Shauna's neighborhood. Once inside, he would have to pass close to nearly a dozen other homes to reach the one he was looking for, but if tomorrow night was rainy like this, he doubted that would be particularly difficult. Satisfied that things on the ground here matched the images he'd stored, Eric powered down the phone and put it back in the dry bag. He was stuffing the bag back into the kayak when he suddenly found himself caught in the beam of a powerful light cutting through the foliage from somewhere above him on the bank. Assuming the light might be attached to the barrel of a weapon, Eric was careful not to make any sudden moves as he slowly turned around, his hands visible and out away from his sides. He had been confident that he was alone here, or he wouldn't have risked giving himself away with the illuminated screen of the phone. Now he knew he'd been mistaken, and he was about to learn the price of his error. As he slowly turned to show he was unarmed, the person holding the light finally spoke:

"What are you doing out here in the middle of the night, dude? Don't you know the ICW is under lockdown, even in the daytime?"

The blinding beam locked onto his face and Eric turned his eyes off to one side. He felt like a complete idiot for letting someone get the drop on him, but unless this person was already determined to shoot him, it wasn't over yet, even though he was unarmed at the moment. His M4 carbine, stashed under the front deck of the kayak where he could grab it while padding, was hopelessly out of reach. The Glock 19 he normally wore hidden under his shirt in an appendix holster was in the dry bag with his phone and snacks, as he'd planned on using the rifle if he needed a weapon while on the water. He'd briefly considered keeping it on him before leaving the ship, but decided against it at the last minute, as he didn't expect to be far from the rifle. But even if he had the Glock, he would still be at a disadvantage trying to reach for it while fixed in that beam of light.

As soon as he heard the voice behind the light though, Eric knew he wasn't dealing with a law enforcement officer or soldier. The tone was far too casual for one thing and lacking any semblance of command presence for another. In addition to that, his choice of words told Eric the speaker was probably a lot younger than him. He kept his eyes diverted to avoid ruining his night vision, because the stranger had already taken a couple of steps in his direction. He answered the question in an equally casual tone, as if he had no concern of a possible threat. "No, I wasn't aware of that. I'm just passing through. I'm not from around here."

"Passing through from where? *Everyone* knows about the curfews and restrictions!"

"I didn't. Like I said, I'm not from around here. I've been traveling for a while, paddling down the coast from up north. I'm just trying to find a safe place to lay low and stay out of trouble, that's all. Somewhere down in the Keys, probably."

"Up north? How far up north? Why would you come to south Florida now, after the hurricane? Florida's all messed up. No place in this state is safe, much less this part."

"It's not safe where I was either, and I like warm weather. Living out of a kayak is easier down here."

"Not if they see you it won't be. You won't be living at all because they'll shoot you on sight."

"I don't doubt that. That's why I'm traveling at night. It's not that hard to keep out of sight on a dark night like tonight, with the rain falling."

"Maybe not, but *I* saw you. If I was one of them, you'd be dead already. But I guess I probably wouldn't have seen you if you hadn't stopped here, and if I hadn't already woke up to chase the raccoons away from my camp."

"You're camping here?"

"Yep. I've been here for a little over three weeks. I had to leave my apartment because it was too dangerous to stay after the lights went out, and besides, there's nothing to eat in the city. Nobody's seen me here yet, but it's just a matter of time before they do. I can hear people talking from the road just through those woods every day. I need to get out of here soon and find a better hideout."

Eric could care less about this stranger's situation, but he was pissed at himself for being so stupid. He thought he'd checked well enough before pulling up to the bank to get out, but this fellow had obviously seen him first and had frozen in place in the dark undergrowth. Even with night vision, Eric had missed him.

"It looks like that kayak has two seats," he went on. "How about we team up and I go with you to the Keys? I can paddle a kayak as well as anybody and I know my way around down there. I know the perfect place to go. And I'm good at getting by off of fishing and scavenging, so you don't have to worry about that. I can show you a trick or two when it comes to fishing. I've been fishing these waters all my life."

"I'm sorry, but I can't do that. My boat's already too full of gear. There's no room for you and your stuff."

"What kind of gear? Why do you need all that gear for just one person? Let me see what you've got in there!"

Eric saw the stranger's light sweep his kayak from bow to stern as he took another step closer. Watching with his peripheral vision to avoid being blinded, Eric could now see that he was waving it back and forth in his hand, and that it wasn't mounted to a gun barrel. He had something in his other hand though that he was keeping out of sight, holding it back behind him in the shadows. Eric had little doubt that it was a weapon, and he intended to maintain his distance.

"Look! You need to stay back. I can't take you with me and I can't help you. I'm in a hurry to move on, so you can go back to your camp now and I'll just be on my way. I'm sorry I disturbed you."

"Yeah right! You could, but you just don't want to, probably because you're an asshole. Look, I've been stuck here because somebody stole *my* boat while I was asleep. I offered to help you out, but if that's not going to work, then you don't leave me a lot of choice, because I *need* that kayak. But I'll give you a chance to just leave it where it is and hit the road. I don't want to hurt anybody, I really don't, but everybody's got to do what they gotta do to survive, man."

Three

AS HE MADE HIS threat, the stranger turned the light slightly so that Eric could see that he was holding a long machete in his other hand, the blade down and behind him, but ready to bring into action. The light also revealed that he was wiry and scruffy-looking from living out in the woods, but quite young, just as Eric had deduced from his voice. His biggest mistake was not taking Eric's head off before opening his mouth. That told Eric all he needed to know about his would-be opponent's lack of combat experience and the threat level he presented.

"Okay, okay! You win! Just put that thing down, I don't want trouble," Eric said. "But please, just let me get a couple of my bags out of there. You can have the rest."

Eric took a step towards his boat, watching out of the corner of his eye as he turned to the side and moved to reach into the kayak's cockpit. The kid stepped down the bank to follow him, brandishing the big blade, confident that he had the upper hand. Eric let him get closer as he pretended to focus on getting his stuff. He could have easily grabbed the

Glock out of the dry bag and shot him in the face before he took the final step that would put him in machete range. The thieving punk probably deserved it but Eric didn't want to risk drawing attention to the waterway with unnecessary gunfire. Besides, his double-ended kayak paddle was propped at an angle across the deck in front him, within easy reach. Without hesitation, Eric quickly grabbed it with both hands, pivoting on his feet in the soft mud as he put his entire weight into a sudden thrust, driving the tapered end of the carbon fiber blade hard into his opponent's midsection. The Greenland-style paddle doubled nicely as a fighting staff, and Eric had practiced with it for that purpose many times. With its narrowly tapered blade surfaces that were much thicker and stiffer than those of typical kayak paddles, it was a formidable weapon. Eric heard the satisfying expulsion of breath as his single thrust took the wind and the fight out of the kid, his machete and flashlight falling into the edge of the water as he went down. Eric swept up the machete in one hand and threw it out of reach into the mangroves as he stood over his fallen assailant. Then he drew the Glock from his bag and pressed the barrel hard against the side of the kid's face.

"Listen up, punk. I'm letting you live only because I just got home and I'm not ready to start killing people yet, but let this be a lesson for future reference! I don't know who you are or what you've been doing since the shit hit the fan here, but playing pirate is a good way to get dead real fast! I didn't like doing it, but I've put away more Somali thugs younger than you plying that trade than I care to count, and *they* had AKs and RPGs, not machetes. I would stick to the fishing and scavenging if I were you, kid!"

"I'm sorry man, I didn't know...."

"No, you didn't know did you? You didn't know you picked the wrong guy this time did you bud? But it's your lucky night anyway, because you're still breathing!"

"Barely...." He was gasping, trying to get his breath back as he lay there doubled-up in pain.

This wasn't the first time a would-be assailant had tested Eric in a dark place and paid for his mistake with a hard life lesson. Eric wasn't as obviously imposing as some of the guys he'd worked with, but more than one challenger had found out the hard way that it wasn't always possible to judge a fighter on appearance alone. Standing right at six feet even and weighing a solid 180 pounds, his lean physique didn't particularly draw attention under normal clothing, but Eric was all muscle and sinew, and knew how to use it.

"I'm sorry, man. I just messed up. I wish I'd never spoken to you now. You would have never known I was here."

"It's too late for that now, but you can help me out with some local intel since we're already having this conversation.

Let's just forget about what just happened and start all over, how about that? What's your name anyway? I'm Eric."

"It's Jonathan. I don't know what I could tell you that you probably don't already know."

"No, you're wrong there, Jonathan. Almost anything would be useful, because the truth is, I didn't really come from up north. I just reached the coast here less than an hour ago. I haven't been in the U.S. in more than a year, since long before everything fell apart, so I need you to fill me in. I need to know the situation on the ground here, so I'll know what I'm up against."

"Why? What are you planning on doing? What do you mean you just reached the coast? Reached it from where?"

"From Africa," Eric said. "Actually the Canary Islands off the coast of Africa, but that's close enough."

"Not in *that?*" Jonathan nodded at the kayak.

"No, but it's how I got ashore from a bigger ship. Anyway, none of that matters. I'm here to find my ex-wife and my daughter, if they're still here. And after that, my father, who lives over near the Gulf Coast, on the other side of the state."

"You've got your work cut out for you then, dude. I'd hate to be looking for anyone I cared about around here. It's dangerous as hell out there on the roads."

"Which is why I'm not on them. I can reach my ex-wife's house by water; and my father's place too, it'll just take a lot longer. Are you from around here? Have you been down around North Palm Beach since the hurricane?"

"I used to live not too far south of there, so yeah, I came that way to get here. I was planning on going farther north, but I like this spot and the fishing has been good."

"The house I'm looking for is on a network of canals right off the ICW. The community is gated from the road, from what I understand, so I'm hoping it will still be secure."

"Gates don't mean shit. They can't keep out the mobs that have been going through all those neighborhoods, especially now. Most of the rich people that lived in places like that have left since the hurricane, or at least tried to if they could still get out."

"Left to go where?"

"I don't know. The ones that still had gas probably tried to drive somewhere north of all the damage."

"What about the checkpoints and roadblocks? I heard that the highways all over the country were restricted long before the storm hit."

"They were, so I don't know where they went. Maybe there's a shelter set up for them somewhere. I've heard rumors, but nobody knows the truth."

"So who's in charge of all that here? Is it the National Guard? The Army? Are the local police and sheriff departments still operating?"

"Dude, that's a lot of questions I can't answer. Yeah, I've seen soldiers… not as many as before the hurricane… but some. I don't know who they are, but I know you don't want them to see you trying to go anywhere. That's why I'm hiding out. It's the best way I know to avoid trouble. I've heard a lot of shooting since I've been here. Most of it in the daytime and most of it kind of far away, but I have no idea what it was about."

What Jonathan was telling him was about what Eric expected. Aside from the hurricane situation here, he was sure that there was something like martial law in effect in many places, at least wherever the authorities were trying to maintain control. If some of the rumors were true though, there were many other regions where they had essentially given up for now.

"What can you tell me about the riots and the fighting going on before the hurricane? Have you been anywhere outside of Florida since all that started?"

"No, I hardly ever leave Florida. I had to work all the time before, but when the banks shut down, I quit like everybody else. I mean, what was the point if we weren't going to get paid? I didn't have much money, but I had a little cash on me, and I had my boat. That's how I got here."

"You really had a boat? I thought you were bullshitting me. Where is it now?'

"Stolen, like I said! I had it hidden right there where you pulled up in your kayak. Somebody took it the second night I was here. I never heard or saw anything, but luckily, I had most of my fishing gear up there in the bushes where I set up camp, so they didn't get that."

"So you figured you'd just take my kayak then, since someone stole your boat, right?"

"Look, I'm sorry man. I didn't know who you were or what you were doing here. As far as I knew, you could have taken it from someone else before you stopped here. I screwed up. What can I say?"

"Don't worry about it. That's history now. So, back to the situation before the hurricane; were there major riots and shootings here in this part of Florida?"

"Oh yeah, there was all kind of crap going on! It started within days after the soldiers killed all those armed protesters in Los Angeles. That shit broke out in Miami the very next day, and the riots there were probably as bad as any in the country. I heard they burned down half the city and hundreds of people got killed. It was bad in Tampa and Orlando too, and then it started spreading to just about every town, even West Palm Beach, where I used to live. It got to the point where most people weren't even going to work anymore, and it sure wasn't safe to be out at night. It was like a freakin' war zone in a lot of places, especially the big cities, right up until the hurricane hit. For all I know, they're still fighting wherever there are enough people left."

"And this sort of thing was happening all over the United States to some extent, right?"

"Yeah, it was pretty much everywhere. Up north, out west, you name it. I'm sure it was worse in places like California, but it wasn't long before it was hard to even get the news. They started cutting off TV broadcasts and even the Internet and cell phone networks for days at a time, and then eventually for good."

"Who, the federal government?"

"I guess. Whoever was in control, but who knows who that is now? How were we supposed to know anything with no news and no way to communicate?"

"I'm sure that it was a calculated effort to suppress networking among the insurrectionists. You said the banks and other means of transferring funds shut down shortly after that, right?"

"Yep, but you couldn't buy much of anything even if you *could* get money out. The stores were sold out of everything. Gas stations ran out of gas. That led to more riots and more people getting shot. The only ones not affected as bad were people living out in the country where it wasn't as crowded and people like me here on the coast that had a boat and the know-how to catch fish, especially after the hurricane. I was pretty lucky in the beginning, at least until I lost my boat. Now, I'm stuck, and it sucks big time."

"You're still better off than most people here from what you're telling me. Now I'm *really* worried about my daughter, and my ex. I had hoped things had been quieter here in Palm Beach County before the storm hit, but from what you're telling me, they were in danger then too. I have no idea if they stayed here through all that or if they decided to get out either before or after the hurricane; *if* they were able to get out at all."

"How old is you're daughter? Is she little?"

"No. She's nearly twenty now. She's a student at a university in Colorado."

"Nearly twenty? You don't *even* look old enough to have a twenty-year-old daughter, man. Heck, I just turned twenty myself. I figured you were about thirty."

"Add another decade and some change," Eric laughed. "Anyway, she's a young woman now, but that doesn't mean I'm not worried about her. I don't know if she was even back in Florida when the hurricane hit, but she should have been home for summer break if she was able to travel from Colorado."

"Man, where have you been for so long that you don't even know? That's pretty messed up, dude!"

"Like I said, I just got in from overseas. I've been working in Sweden and Norway most recently, but lots of other places before that."

"Doing what? It's worse over there in Europe than it is here, from what I've heard. I'm surprised you could find a job."

"Security contracting. It's in demand everywhere now. There's no shortage of jobs in my line of work."

"Oh wow, so that's what you meant when you said that about those Somali pirates. You weren't kidding, were you? You're like a *mercenary!* I remember seeing a lot of stuff about you guys working in Iraq and Afghanistan on the news, years ago. I'll bet you make a shitload of money, don't you?"

"The pay is good, but that's not all there is to it. Most of the time I feel like I'm making a difference. And there's a lot more freedom than when I was in the Navy."

"The Navy? Where you a freakin' Navy SEAL? *That's* where I've seen a kayak like that! Some movie where the SEALS used them to sneak in and blow up enemy ships in some harbor somewhere! Man, I really fucked up didn't I? I should be dead right now, trying to steal a kayak from a freakin' Navy SEAL turned mercenary pirate hunter!"

"It's all good, Jonathan. We all make mistakes, and I made the first one. I'm the one who should be dead. If you were one of the *real* troublemakers around here and were properly armed, you'd have blown me away before I knew what hit me!"

"I *wish* I had a gun! I used to have a .38 Special I kept in my car all the time, but it got stolen when somebody broke into it back when I was still working."

"Well, you've had some bad luck with thieves, haven't you, Jonathan?"

"Yeah, I guess I really have, come to think of it."

Eric twisted his wrist to activate the backlighting on the dial of his dive watch. With less than an hour until daybreak, he was running out of time to get situated for the day. If Jonathan had managed to stay hidden here for weeks, Eric figured this was as good a spot as any he might find nearby. Now that they'd talked and cleared up things between them, Eric wasn't worried that the kid would try any more tricks. He could pick his brain for more info while he waited, and then he would set out for Shauna's tonight after getting some rest.

Four

JONATHAN SEEMED DELIGHTED WHEN Eric announced his plans. He had no doubt been starving for conversation, hiding out in the mangroves as he'd been doing. He was greatly impressed with Eric too after their little misunderstanding, and was eager to hear more about the life of a professional military security contractor.

"Hey, I'll help you with that," he said, as Eric pulled the bow of his kayak higher up the bank.

"Thanks, but that's far enough. I'll cover it up with a few leafy branches before daybreak so it won't be visible from the waterway, but I've got too much crap in there to unload it all and get it completely out of the water."

"What in the hell did you put in here? It feels like it weighs a ton!" Jonathan said, as he tried to lift the bow himself.

"Just stuff I figured I'd need. I came here knowing I couldn't count on getting resupplied anytime soon, and knowing I'd better be ready for anything."

With that, Eric reached under the foredeck of the kayak from the cockpit and pulled out his M4, slipping an arm through the sling to free up his hands for carrying more of his stuff into the woods.

"Whoa, dude! Whatcha got there? That's a cool-looking AR-15!"

"Yeah, but it's not the kind you can go pick up at the sporting goods store."

"No shit? Is it the real deal? Is it fully automatic? Can I see it?"

"Later. It'll be light soon enough. I want to get everything I need out of here and cover up this boat right now."

"I'll help you carry it! Just hand me some stuff. My camp is about 50 yards back in the woods there. You don't have to worry about being seen back in there. And with *that*, it won't matter if you are. You can just blow somebody's shit away!"

It wasn't hard to figure out that Jonathan's knowledge of firearms came from too much TV. But at least he knew how to fish and had sense enough to find a good hideout, two things that no doubt contributed to him making it this long. Eric knew most kids his age wouldn't have a clue what do in a situation like this, but before he let his thoughts go there, he had to stop. His own Megan was in that category, as much as it pained him to acknowledge it. He knew a lot of that was his fault, and he'd tried to teach her what he could the few times he'd had a chance, but that had been a long time ago. The eager 10-year-old that he taught to shoot and even took camping two or three times soon became the rebellious teen that didn't want to hear anything he had to say. Eric knew a lot of that was because he hadn't been there for her in those critical years, but there was nothing he could do to change that now. All he could hope was that he'd get a second chance. She might not want it, but she was going to *need* his help now.

When he'd gotten the things he needed out of the kayak, Eric fished Jonathan's machete out of the mangroves where he'd tossed it, and used it to cut a few branches to hide the boat. Then he handed it back to him and shook his head.

"That thing's dull as shit."

"I know. I don't have anything to sharpen it with. I had a file but it was with my tools in the boat when it got stolen."

Eric said nothing but he knew he would end up putting an edge on Jonathan's blade while they talked. He didn't know exactly why, but he liked this kid despite his attempt to take his boat. It was probably because of his determination to survive, and the fact that he was successfully doing it on his own, living off of his fishing instead of looting or looking for a handout. The sudden opportunity to take a seaworthy kayak had caused him a brief lapse in judgment, but Eric could forgive him once, and while he was here, he would help him out if he could.

As dawn broke over the waterway, the rain picked up a bit and Eric followed Jonathan to his hidden camp, where he had rigged up a camouflaged poly tarp over the small fire pit where he had been cooking his meals. A cheap dome tent that he had been sleeping in was pitched nearby. Leaning up against the surrounding trees were several fishing rods, and hanging from a low branch was a cast net.

"This is home for me, at least for now. I guess I'll be staying here until someone else finds my camp. If I still had my boat, I'd have probably moved on by now."

"There's advantages to moving and advantages to staying," Eric said. "I'd say you're pretty well set as long as the fishing is good. You don't know who you might run into out there on the water."

"I know. My boat had a motor, but it was just a 25-horse Mercury, so it wasn't fast. I think your kayak is a lot better even if you have to paddle. It's hard to see, especially at night and it doesn't make a sound. That thing is badass! Is it specially made for the SEALs?"

"Not really. It's the manufacturer's 'military' model, but anyone can buy one. Special Ops units rarely use them these days. They've got much more sophisticated high-tech delivery systems for the most part, but they can come in handy for some coastal and river work for reconnaissance and things like that. On one of my more recent contract jobs we used them that way. We'd sink them when we got close to shore so they wouldn't be found while we were carrying out the mission. They're slow and kind of primitive, but they have a lot of advantages, like the silence you mentioned, plus the ability to carry several hundred pounds of gear and explosives."

"Wow! Is that what you've got in there now? Is that why it's so heavy, because of all the grenades and shit?"

Eric smiled. He didn't know if he should admit it or not, but yes, he did have a few grenades. They were readily available when he was putting together his gear list for the trip, so why not? But the grenades only accounted for a tiny percentage of his payload on this mission. What he had more of was food and other essentials for an extended solo operation without resupply, including of course, lots of ammo. There was another select-fire M4 stashed in a dry bag under the stern deck, along with a mounted M203 grenade launcher and a couple dozen M406 high-explosive rounds for it. Eric also had a spare Glock 19 and plenty of extra magazines for the pairs of handguns and rifles. He planned to do his best to avoid getting into a situation where he would need his weapons, but he wasn't coming here without backups and sufficient ammo. Eric knew too that if he was intercepted and caught by the authorities the consequences would be severe. If things were like they'd been in France and Italy when he'd worked there, just having the weapons would probably get him summarily executed. Nevertheless, he deemed it worth the risk.

Jonathan told him what he knew of the situation, but unfortunately, that was not a lot, as the kid hadn't been outside the local area. Eric would find out more as he went along, hopefully getting the details straight from Shauna and Megan soon. As they sat there under the tarp while the rain drummed down, the world beyond Jonathan's hidden camp seemed unnaturally quiet. There was no traffic moving on the nearby road, just as there had been none on the bridge Eric passed beneath in the dark. No voices reached their ears over the sound of the rain, nor were there any of the gunshots Jonathan said he heard most days. It was impossible to know if it was the weather keeping people from moving about, or if there were simply fewer people remaining with each passing day. Thinking of all the possibilities made the hours drag by for Eric. He wanted to get to Shauna's house *now* and find out if she and Megan were okay.

If he hadn't been intimately familiar with south Florida weather patterns from living here in years past, Eric would have been tempted to move on under the cover of the rain. But knowing how fast things changed here, he wouldn't risk it. The sun could come out again before he was halfway there and then he'd be stuck, looking for another place to hide, because there was no way he was going to risk paddling down the waterway in broad daylight and good weather. He resigned himself to a long day of waiting under Jonathan's tarp, and to pass the time he worked on the dull machete, first with a small file and then with the water stones he carried for his knives.

"That's a lot better," he said, as he tested the edge by shaving a small patch of hair off his forearm. "I would say be careful with it, but back when I was a kid in the Boy Scouts, they taught us that a sharp blade is safer than a dull one."

"That's freakin' awesome!" Jonathan said, as he felt the edge.

"It'll stay that way a while if you don't hit any rocks or anything like that with it."

Eric touched up his fighting knife after finishing Jonathan's machete. It was a custom seven-inch Bowie blade with rosewood scales; given to him by a fellow teammate whose life he'd saved when he was wounded in a firefight with the Taliban. Drew Herrington would never walk again, but he was still able to pursue his blade craft when he got home. He had presented the knife to him years later, when Eric had gone to visit him at his father's ranch in Texas.

"That's a badass knife!" Jonathan said, when Eric handed it to him to let him see. "Ever killed anybody with it? How many people *have* you killed?"

Eric just smiled and ignored the question.

"I'll bet it was a lot, huh? The wars in Europe have been bad. Worse than what you saw in Iraq and Afghanistan, huh?"

"Yeah, it was bad. It's been bad everywhere, and unfortunately, now here."

"Do you think things will ever calm down? I mean it seems like the more the government tries to do, like shutting down the roads and airports and all, the more fighting it causes. It's like a freakin' civil war, I guess. I wonder how many people will have to die before it all stops?"

"There's no telling, but if you get involved in it, you'll die sooner, I can assure you of that."

"Well, it looks like *you're* prepared to get involved."

"No. I'm prepared to *survive.* All I care about is getting my daughter out of this mess, and then my father. If my ex wants to come with us, she can come too, but she's got a new husband and a stepson, so I don't know how all that would work out. All I know is that we're getting out. It's up to them what they want to do."

"I hear you, man. Divorce complicates the shit out of things. But even if it's just you and your daughter and your dad, where would you go to get away from all this?"

"Lots of places, just not anywhere in the U.S. We'll get a boat once we get to my father's place on the Caloosahatchee. He owns a boatyard over there and I'm sure he can line us up with something big enough to sail far away from all this insanity."

"A sailboat? Yeah, I guess that would work, if you can get away from land before you get blown out of the water. At least you won't need fuel, and that's a good thing because it's damned hard to get if you can get any at all."

"Even if it wasn't for the fuel problem, sailing is the only thing feasible for the kind of distances that would do any good."

"So you're talking like getting the fuck completely out of this whole part of the world, huh? Like crossing the ocean and shit? Where would you go? Somewhere like New Zealand? I guess that would be safe, huh?"

"Maybe. But there's lots of out of the way places you can reach with a good boat. The main thing is getting away from the U.S. mainland, and staying away from Europe, the Mediterranean, the Red Sea, and Persian Gulf… all the usual hot spots. I've seen all of that part of the world I need to see in this lifetime."

"Man, it sounds like you've got a solid plan. I hope it works out for you, I really do. I wish I could say I had a plan, but I really don't. I'm just taking it day-by-day right now, you know what I mean?"

"I am too, Jonathan. All that stuff is way out there in the abstract future right now. First, I have to find my daughter, and then my father. That might be the hard part, but it's also the only part that matters right now. I'll worry about the rest of it when the time comes."

Five

As THE LONG RAINY day wore on into afternoon, Eric followed Jonathan through the woods to his most productive fishing spots, where he worked his lures among the submerged root systems until he had a couple of nice mangrove snappers. Jonathan had been doing all of his cooking over a small fire pit under the tarp, and because of the daily rains, he had stashed a supply of dry twigs and larger branches under there and in a corner of his tent.

Eric saw that despite Jonathan's youth and lack of fighting experience, he was a pretty good outdoorsman who knew how to stay fed and comfortable in the wild. He had not been lying about that when he'd first suggested Eric take him with him before threatening him with the machete. The fire he rekindled to cook the fish was just large enough to get the job done but no more, creating minimal smoke that might filter through the trees and be visible from the road. As the flames burned the wood down to cooking coals, Jonathan expertly gutted and filleted the fish before laying them out on a small wire grill that he carried as part of his camping kit.

"Where'd you learn so much about fishing and camping, Jonathan?"

"From my dad. We fished almost every day in the summer, and went camping anytime he had a long weekend off. Sometimes we went down to the Keys, and other times over to the Everglades. That was my favorite. Man, there's some good fishing over there, but the camping is tough, because the mosquitos will eat you alive. The Everglades is one place you don't want to go in the summer! We usually went when I was out of school for Christmas and Spring Break."

"Where is he now?"

"My dad? He died a couple of years ago."

"I'm sorry to hear that. It sounds like he taught you a lot while you had him."

Jonathan said nothing else about it, so Eric didn't ask him any more questions. He figured if his mother or other family members were still here he would mention it, but since he didn't, that probably meant they were not. When they had eaten their fill of fish, Eric opened one of the dry bags he had brought to Jonathan's camp from the kayak and dumped the contents onto the ground. This was one of two such bags that contained his quick energy, eat-on-the-go fuels: including things like almonds, peanuts, dried fruit and energy bars. If he got into a situation where he needed to eat while paddling, these snacks would keep him going until he could prepare a more substantial meal later. He had plenty of MREs and some canned goods stashed away deeper in the kayak, as he didn't come here counting on being able to resupply along the way. Since Jonathan had shared his shelter and his fish with him, Eric insisted he take some of the snack foods to add some variety to his diet.

"You know, since you brought it up earlier, I've been thinking about those trips to the Everglades with my dad," Jonathan said. "No matter how bad the mosquitos get at times, that would be a pretty good place to hang out about now, with the way things are. Anybody that's good at fishing could do all right over there."

"You'd have to get inland from the mangroves though to find a fresh water supply, right?" Eric knew a bit about the Everglades. He had done some canoeing there with one of his buddies back before he joined the Navy, when he was a bit younger than Jonathan. He remembered that there was no fresh water to be had along the route they'd paddled, just mile after mile of mangrove forest submerged in brackish water.

"Yeah, up the rivers is where you find the best hideouts anyway, way up in the sawgrass marsh on the little hardwood hammocks that are scattered all over. We used to go up one called the Turner River. It was like a jungle up there and the fishing was incredible! But who knows? A bunch of other people may have the same idea and it could be crowded now. I'm just daydreaming anyway, because I don't have a way to get over there or a boat to get back to the good spots anyway."

Eric could understand Jonathan's dilemma, but he didn't have a suggestion for him. Trying to cross the Florida peninsula on the roads wouldn't be a good idea at all, and even if he had a boat that could make the trip, it was a long haul to the Everglades, either rounding the southern tip of the state through the Keys or going north to the Indian River to cross by way of Lake Okeechobee. Eric had been thinking of these options already, because he knew that he was going to eventually have to use one or the other of them to get to his father's place. Bart Branson owned a boatyard on the Caloosahatchee River between the lake and the Gulf Coast, and either route to get there had its drawbacks. How and when Eric would do it depended entirely on what he found when he reached Shauna's house, but he wasn't planning to leave Florida without his father. The real problem though was going to be talking Bart Branson into leaving. The old man was stubborn and set in his ways, and like Eric's brother, Keith, he loved where he lived and the work he did. Things would have to be at least as bad as Eric guessed that they were to get him to even consider giving it up.

"I'll probably hang out here another week or two unless the fishing dries up," Jonathan went on, snapping Eric out of his thoughts of his father again. "I guess I can do like you, and travel at night if I decide to move on. I can go north up towards Hobe Sound."

"If I remember right, there are quite a few parks and natural areas along the ICW between here and there."

"Yeah, and since I'll be going on foot, it should be better than going south, at least if I can get past Tequesta and all the other developed areas. I'll just have to play it by ear and see. Right now though, I guess I'll just hang tight here while I can."

When it was dark again, Jonathan showed Eric where he had been getting his fresh water. Just across the road from his wooded hideout, there was an office building with a large ornamental fountain barely visible among the landscaping of palms and shrubbery. The fountain was no longer running, of course, but the deep circular pool around it was full, and the water was relatively clean. Jonathan hadn't been treating it, because he didn't have the means to do so, but he had not gotten sick so far. Drinking surface water was always a risk, but Eric figured it was probably as good or better than the water other survivors in the area had access to. Eric had brought his own supply of drinking water in several 10-liter bladder tanks distributed in the bilges of the kayak. He had an iodine purification system to treat more when he needed it, but none to offer Jonathan, so he didn't mention it. All things considered, the kid was surviving just fine on his own before Eric came along and would likely continue to do so.

"It looks like the rain is going to hold out for you, dude," Jonathan said, as he helped Eric carry his bags back to the kayak. "You should be able to get there without being seen. At least I hope so. After what I know about you now, I'd kind of feel sorry for any dumbass like me that tries to give you trouble."

Eric laughed and shook Jonathan's hand. "Thanks man. I'm glad I stopped here after all and I'm glad you got the drop on me. You might have saved my life without even knowing it, because I won't make that mistake again, you can bet on that!"

"I hope you find your daughter, dude. I really do."

"Me too, Jonathan. Good luck with the fishing. Keep staying out of sight and I think you'll be fine."

With that, Eric slid back into the cockpit of his kayak and used the paddle to push it stern first back out of the narrow channel as Jonathan stood there watching. It was an interesting encounter that could have turned out far different than it had. As it was, Eric was really glad he'd restrained himself in the face of Jonathan's threat. It would have been a shame if he'd seriously maimed or even killed him, because it was now obvious that he wasn't surviving by taking advantage of others despite the temptation of Eric's sea kayak. The whole thing could have turned out far worse for either of them, but if nothing else, it served to remind Eric that he was going to have to be on top of his game every minute he was here. He had no way of knowing how many there might be, but it made sense that there would be other refugees living in the mangroves and many of them might prove far more dangerous than Jonathan.

As he paddled back into the ICW and turned south, Eric was determined to keep his distance from the banks on either side whether or not the shoreline was developed. The rain made him more comfortable with this option, as it was heavy enough to screen him from view of anyone who might happen to be near the waterway at this time of night. He paddled as quietly as possible, dipping the blades on each stroke so that they barely made a sound. Silence was another advantage of the Greenland style paddle. With proper technique, the long, narrow blades made little disturbance upon entry into the water. The design was perfect, developed by ancient hunters who depended on stealth to approach their wary prey from the water. The paddle was also efficient for long distance travel, as the blades got just enough bite with each stroke for easy propulsion without causing undue strain on the joints of the paddler's wrists and elbows. As he used it to cruise south at an average speed of three and a half knots, Eric couldn't help thinking about how well his sudden thrust with it had worked to disarm Jonathan. A slight change in angle, targeting the throat, would have easily killed him. The time he'd spent working with the paddle practicing his staff forms had certainly paid off, and Eric made a mental note to keep it up whenever he had the chance.

He had passed under another bridge a short distance south of Jonathan's camp, and now after traveling another hour and a half, he was approaching a second one. Seeing it told him that he was close. Once he was south of that overpass, the entrance to Shauna's neighborhood was just a little over a mile and half to the south. He stayed to the middle of the channel and slipped under the bridge as quickly as possible. On the south side he passed the entrance to another marina that appeared abandoned since the hurricane. From what he could see in the dark through the rain, many of the vessels docked there had broken their mooring lines, smashing into each other and against the pilings. A sailboat mast leaning at a sharp angle was entangled in the rigging of a neighboring boat, and a large motor yacht was lying on its side at the edge of the entrance channel. The damage here seemed worse than it was just a few mile north at Jupiter Inlet, but Eric knew that the microbursts of winds associated with hurricanes could do strange things like that. And since the eye of the storm had made landfall somewhere to the south, he knew too that the damage would only get worse farther on in that direction.

The final stretch of the ICW between the marina and his turn-off took him past blacked-out waterfront homes along both banks, all of them obviously damaged and probably abandoned. Seeing all this destruction deflated what little hope he had left of finding Megan and Shauna at home here. Surely they had gotten out before things got so bad, but he had to go there anyway to be certain. He checked his watch again when he reached the canal entrance that he'd memorized. He had nearly five hours of darkness remaining, but he doubted now that he would have to wait until dawn to get his answers, because it was unlikely anyone was there at all, much less asleep.

Six

ERIC ENTERED THE MAIN canal, paddling west a hundred yards before coming to the intersection of a north-south canal that appeared just as it had on his satellite images. He turned right, heading north for a short distance to the next turn-off, and then paddled down a smaller canal leading farther west. The storm-battered houses here had been expensive and luxurious, but packed into every available space that would afford their owners access to the waterfront. Each had its own dock, most badly damaged by the storm surge, and the only boats still here were the few that were small enough to be hoisted clear of the water on mechanical lifts. Presumably, any larger vessels that had been moored in the canal were either moved before the storm by their owners or stolen by the looters that came afterwards.

Meticulously landscaped lawns with their plantings of exotic tropical plants and palms were now knee-high in weeds. Many of the tallest palms had been uprooted or stripped of their fronds and fruit by hurricane-force winds that turned hanging clusters of green coconuts into deadly projectiles. Despite that damage, most of the vegetation was thriving in the aftermath and seeing the rampant growth reminded Eric of similar scenes in the tropics where the jungle quickly swallowed the abandoned endeavors of man. Nature would take over again here too, and with no one around to beat it back, it wouldn't take long.

The rain had let up to a soft drizzle now, so Eric was doubly cautious to keep his paddle strokes quiet and to stop and drift often, listening for signs of life. The house he was looking for was the last one on the north bank of this smaller canal, in what was essentially a cul-de-sac from this waterborne approach. As he paddled past the last of the neighboring houses, he could see the hurricane shutters still in place on most of the windows, but he also saw that some had apparently been broken into, as evidenced by doors standing wide open or broken completely off their hinges.

When he reached the dock that he knew was Daniel Hartfield's, Eric couldn't see the back door because a high stucco privacy wall around the swimming pool blocked his view from where he sat so low on the water. He had been expecting this because he knew the pool was there from the satellite imagery. The 18-foot center-console runabout that Shauna had mentioned they owned was missing, but Eric hadn't really expected it to be there considering all the other empty docks he'd already passed. He swept his night vision monocular across what he could see of the yard and the house, but there was no sign that it was occupied. The house situated directly across the canal appeared to be abandoned too, its sliding glass back door shattered either by the storm or the looters.

Eric quietly placed his paddle on the dock beside him and reached for his M4, slipping the sling over his head before pulling himself up to a crouch to step out of the kayak. Once he was on the dock, he leaned over and shoved the kayak beneath it with the paddle inside, tying it off to a piling under there so it would stay put and out of sight. Keeping low and moving quickly, Eric crossed to the wall in back of the pool and crouched in the shadows of a line of oleander bushes planted alongside it. From there, he crept along the wall to the iron gate at the side entrance, where he had a view of the pool and the entrance to the screen room attached to the back of the house.

When he was sure there was no one around, getting inside the pool area was easy enough. Eric grabbed the top of the seven-foot wall and pulled himself up with both arms until he could plant a foot next to one hand, and then it was a simple matter to vault to the ground within. The metal-framed entrance door to the screen room was unlocked, so Eric opened it quietly and stepped inside. Holding the slung carbine at the ready with his right hand on the trigger and the muzzle pointing at the entrance, he tested the back door handle with his left hand, finding it unlocked as well.

Eric already knew that Shauna and her family weren't here, with the rest of the neighborhood apparently deserted and the back door unlocked like that. He quickly cleared the house one room at a time to make sure no one else had taken up residence in there after finding the front door open, the casing on the lock side busted apart. Once he was sure he was alone, Eric had a closer look around each room with a small LED headlamp he turned to its dimmest setting. The house had clearly been ransacked. Every drawer in the kitchen had been pulled out and thrown on the floor, along with all the cookware and dishes in the cabinets. Anything edible had been taken, but the floors were smeared with the dried contents of broken jars looters had probably dropped in their haste and frozen foods that had thawed out and spoiled shortly after the power went out.

A side door from the kitchen opened into the enclosed garage, and Eric discovered that both bays were still occupied. The silver Audi A7 sedan that was probably Daniel's and the black BMW Z4 roadster that he knew was Shauna's were both sitting low on the cement floor, their tires slashed and their windshields shattered. As far as he knew, Megan still didn't own a car because she didn't want one, despite the fact that Daniel could have bought her any model she chose. So seeing the two cars here didn't tell him whether his daughter had come home for the summer, but it did tell him Shauna and whoever was here with her must have left by some other means when they got out. It also told him that the break-in likely occurred since then, after the storm when cars were pretty much useless because of the lack of gas and the dangers of the road. The looters, having no use for luxury cars, had simply destroyed them for the hell of it.

Though he looked carefully in every room, Eric found no evidence of blood or any other indicators of a violent attack here, so he felt confident no one had been home when the house was ransacked. Finding the cars still there but the boat missing made him wonder if perhaps they'd used it as a means of escape. Anything was possible, but though he searched for clues he couldn't find anything conclusive. There was so much stuff scattered all over the floors throughout the house that it was impossible to tell if Shauna and her family had packed enough essential possessions to leave. Eric figured that they had though, and that they had probably been forced to leave most of their stuff behind to travel light. He hoped it meant that they had gone to his father's place on the Caloosahatchee. Shauna would know that was a good idea because they had sought shelter there years before during another hurricane when they lived in Boca Raton. Eric knew that his father would welcome them there, even Shauna's new husband. All of this was speculation though until he had more to go on, so Eric continued looking.

The one room he spent the most time in was the bedroom that was obviously Megan's, judging by the girl's clothing on the floor and the posters hanging on the walls. Most of what he saw in there seemed to be relics and mementos of a teenager's years long before she was old enough to move off to college. It didn't appear that she'd occupied the room recently but Eric was looking for evidence that she'd been back for the summer break before Shauna and Daniel evacuated. His first thought was to look for things she would have brought with her from the university, like textbooks or notebooks—anything to let him know she'd been here, but he found nothing of the kind. The looters had scattered her books, old stuffed animals and other keepsakes all over the floor as they emptied the closets and dresser drawers looking for anything of value. Nothing he saw among the mess looked like the things a nineteen-year-old would have use for. The only furniture in the room that wasn't flipped over or broken was the bed, although the covers and pillows had been torn off and tossed aside.

Shining the beam of his light on one of the pillows on the floor next to the bed, something sticking out from beneath it caught Eric's eye. It was a spiral-bound notebook; most of the pages filled with writing that he knew was Megan's hand. He sat on the edge of the bed and flipped through it in the low beam of his headlamp to see if there was anything written recently. There were pages of to-do lists and notes to herself, but the most recent entries appeared to be Christmas shopping lists from the last winter break, when Megan was home for the holidays. He saw nothing in the notebook to indicate she'd written in it before she left again for the spring semester, so disappointed, he put it back on the bed and stood to leave. He knew the lack of hard evidence didn't prove she *hadn't* been here this summer; it was just that there was nothing to prove she had. Had he picked up the pillow completely and looked beneath it, he would have seen another page torn from the notebook that would have told him what he wanted to know. But Eric didn't look there, because something else in the beam of the headlamp caught his eye first.

Bending to pick it up from where he spotted it among the shoes and crumpled T-shirts on the floor, Eric smiled as he felt the smooth curves of the polished black coral carving. It was the likeness of a dolphin, a small work of art he'd bought for her in the Philippines when he'd worked there nearly ten years prior. He unfastened the clasp in the silver rope chain and put it around his neck, tucking the amulet inside his shirt, out of the way. Maybe it didn't mean anything to her now, but she'd worn it all the time when he first gave it to her, and having it around his own neck reminded him of those days when they were so close. After one last look around, he shut the door to Megan's room behind him. He could leave now knowing there was nothing else he needed to look for here, and with only three more hours until daylight returned, it was time to get moving.

It was disappointing to leave without knowing for sure if Megan had made it home from Colorado or not. Since finding her was his primary objective, there was little he could do now other than make his way to his father's place first to see if Shauna and the others were there. In the best-case scenario, they would be and Megan would be there with them. If she wasn't, then Shauna could tell him what she knew. If he couldn't find Shauna, things would be even more complicated. On the one hand, if Megan hadn't returned to Florida at all, then she wouldn't be dealing with all the dangers here in the aftermath of the hurricane. She might be perfectly safe on the campus of the university, or maybe staying with friends somewhere nearby. There were many possibilities, but he wasn't going to find the answers here.

He quietly slipped back out of the house the way he came in, through the screen room to the iron gate by the pool, where stopped to scan the canal. Everything seemed as quiet and deserted as when he arrived, so he exited through the gate this time and slipped back down the dock, where he knelt to reach under the edge for his kayak. Just as he was about to slide back into the cockpit, the sound of outboard motors to the east interrupted the silence. Eric paused to listen. It only took a few seconds to determine that the sound was getting closer, and that's when he realized someone had turned off the ICW and entered the canals. It sounded like more than one boat, and they were both moving fast.

Eric already knew there wasn't a better place to get out of sight on this canal than where he'd already hidden his boat under Daniel and Shauna's dock, so he pushed it back beneath the planking. He quickly realized he wasn't overreacting when to his dismay he saw a speeding runabout round the corner heading into this very cul-de-sac. There was no time to retreat back to the concealment of the fence and surrounding vegetation. He would be spotted if he made a run for it, so instead, Eric lowered himself into the water and ducked under the dock behind his kayak, laying his M4 across the foredeck to keep it out of the water and give him a platform from which to shoot if necessary.

As the driver of the boat realized he entered a dead end canal, he reduced speed but drove the boat all the way to the far end, just past where Eric was hiding. The man didn't stop, but slammed into the wooden seawall with no regard to the damage it did to his boat and quickly scrambled to leap ashore without even bothering to shut off the outboard. Peering out at the other end of the canal, Eric saw why he was in such a hurry. Another boat that was obviously in pursuit rounded the corner and quickly throttled back to idle. Eric saw a man in the bow aiming a rifle as the boat settled down, its wake rolling through the pilings around him and causing the kayak to bounce into the deck boards overhead. A half dozen rifle shots fired in quick succession ripped through the night, and Eric heard a scream from the man ashore as he was struck before he could reach the cover of the nearest house. The fallen man was still alive and trying to crawl, but the other boat was closing the distance, and when the rifle spoke again, Eric saw the victim collapse and remain still.

The pursuing boat was barely twenty yards away from him now, and Eric had it covered in the sights of his rifle. He was certain that he hadn't been seen and doubted the two men aboard it would be looking under any docks, but he was ready to take them out if he had to. Now that he had a close up view of it, he could see that the boat wasn't the typical gloss white fiberglass pleasure craft that was so common here. It was utilitarian aluminum, with a dark, non-reflective gray finish that suggested a law enforcement or military craft, although there were no identifying markings on the hull.

The two men were dressed in dark, nondescript clothing that matched their boat; one standing at the helm while the shooter remained at the bow, focused on the downed man who'd failed to escape them. Eric couldn't be certain they were law enforcement or military, but they didn't look like typical civilians. What he'd just witnessed though seemed more like an execution than an attempt to make an arrest, and further convinced him of the need for stealth while operating in these waters. If he hadn't lucked out with the tide, which was just at the right level to give him sufficient clearance beneath the dock to conceal his kayak, Eric knew he would have been screwed. He didn't want to engage in a firefight with men that might be legitimate law enforcement officers doing their job, but without the kayak and the stuff he had in it, Eric's quest would be finished before it even started. He kept them covered as the boat drifted, it's twin Honda outboards humming at low idle, but as he watched them, he couldn't help thinking of his brother. Keith Branson could be conducting just such a mission this very night, honoring his sworn pledge to protect and serve the people of his jurisdiction. Eric had no way of knowing why they'd killed the fleeing man, but as long as they didn't discover him there, he figured it was none of his business. They were talking in low whispers, but he couldn't hear anything of what was said. The one with the rifle climbed into the other boat and shut off the engine, and as soon as he was back aboard with his partner, the helmsman made a slow U-turn and the mysterious boat headed back out of the canal the way it came.

Eric breathed a sigh of relief as he emerged from under the dock, waiting in the water as he listened to the sound of the boat making its way out of the canal neighborhood and back to the ICW. When the engines finally revved up to cruising speed, he could tell that the two men were heading south, making his next decision easy.

Seven

As Eric settled into his kayak to make his exit, he glanced one more time at the body of the slain man sprawled in the overgrown grass of what once had been a manicured lawn. If what he'd witnessed was indeed a police shooting, justified or otherwise, there was no documentation of it. The men hadn't even bothered to go check the body, and Eric knew there would be no forensics team on the scene to gather evidence or even a coroner to come remove the remains. If they *were* lawmen, it seemed to Eric they were too late to do much good based on what he'd seen of Shauna's neighborhood. It was bizarre to see firsthand what things had come to here in such a short period of time, and once again, Eric found himself hoping he wasn't too late.

He had waited until the sound of the boat had faded away into the distance before getting back in his kayak, and then a bit more in case someone hiding in one of the nearby homes had been drawn out by the sound of gunfire. But nothing moved, and satisfied that he was alone again, he paddled swiftly and silently to escape the network of canals before someone else could arrive. When he came to the final exit, he turned left onto the Intracoastal Waterway, heading north in the direction from which he came. He had done all he could do here and it was time to leave the east coast of Florida behind. He already knew his next destination was his father's place on the Caloosahatchee River; the only question remaining was how, and by which route. Even before he'd left the house and heard the approach of the two boats, he was weighing the pros and cons of the available options in his mind. The most direct route, of course, was overland via the highways or county roads. It was almost a straight shot west across the state that way, as his father's house and boatyard was on approximately the same latitude as Shauna's. There were many problems with that route though, mainly the danger of using roads in a time of lawlessness such as this, especially in a vehicle. If he were traveling light without the need to get his kayak and all that gear overland, Eric could cover the one hundred-mile distance on foot in just a few days. He would have to skirt around towns and other inhabited areas by cutting cross-country, and stay out of sight by traveling at night, but it would be simple and straightforward. But leaving most of his gear and supplies behind wasn't something he was prepared to do considering the challenges he knew he was facing here.

He could get there in the kayak, as his destination was on navigable water; it was just going to take a whole lot longer.

The two route choices began right there at the exit from the canal he'd just left: south down the ICW to Biscayne Bay and around the southern tip of Florida by way of Cape Sable and the Everglades, or north up the ICW to the Indian River and then across the state by way of the Okeechobee Waterway. The western section of the Okeechobee Waterway was actually the Caloosahatchee River that was his destination. It was the shorter route, but there were many obstacles along the way, including several locks that wouldn't likely be in operation. There would be a mix of heavy development and protected nature reserves along either route, although in the current situation there was no way of knowing which would contain the most survivors. The locks and dams he could portage around, but Eric knew that it would probably be impossible to travel that far without encountering others.

He had some thinking to do before making a decision, but his first priority was to get off the water before daybreak. He had turned north for now simply because the boat with the two gunmen had gone south. He would double back if he decided on the southern route, but for now he was headed to where he knew he would find safe haven for the day—at Jonathan's camp near Jupiter Inlet. When he left there he certainly hadn't planned to ever see the kid again, but he hadn't passed a better hideout to spend the coming day between there and Shauna's, so going back was the logical choice, and he knew Jonathan wouldn't mind. The kid would pester him with more questions when he got there, but hopefully he could get some rest and spend part of the coming day working out a plan.

Eric kept his paddle strokes steady and relentless as he headed north in the ICW, glancing over his shoulder occasionally to look for any sign of movement behind him. He made it back to the little cutoff into the mangroves about an hour before dawn, just about the same time as his first arrival there the morning before. Eric doubted Jonathan would be awake and watching this morning, but he didn't want to startle him with his unexpected return. He stopped paddling and let the kayak glide to the sandbar where he'd landed before, whistling a passable imitation of a whippoorwill as he did so. Eric knew that the nocturnal bird inhabited these mangrove sanctuaries, and figured Jonathan wouldn't be alarmed by the sound when he heard it. He stepped out of the kayak and tied it off, repeating the whistle as he slipped through the woods in the direction of the kid's camp. Eric didn't have to worry about getting shot, since he knew Jonathan didn't have any firearms, but when he was close enough for his voice to be heard, he stopped and whispered just loud enough for his voice to carry to the tent.

"Jonathan! It's me. Eric!"

Eric repeated his whippoorwill call and in a moment heard movement inside the tent. Then the zipper opened and once again Eric was blinded by the bright flashlight Jonathan had shone on him the first time they met.

"Get that light out of my face, man! I told you it was me!"

"Dude! I didn't expect to ever see you again! What did you find? Why did you come back?"

"I'll fill you in later—if you don't mind me hanging out here another day."

"Hell no I don't mind! I want to know what happened that made you decide to come back. I want to know what you found!"

"Okay, just let me get my boat covered up again and then I'll get my stuff and we can talk. It'll be daylight again soon, and there *are* people watching the waterway."

A half hour later the two of them were once again sitting under Jonathan's tarp in front of his tent, sharing a meal from Eric's stash.

"Don't be so sure they were lawmen at all," Jonathan said, when Eric told him what he'd witnessed of the two men in the boat. "Just because they didn't look like ordinary looters or thieves don't mean a thing!"

"Well, they didn't go ashore and approach any of the houses. They didn't even take anything out of the dead man's boat or off the body. It looked to me like they were simply pursuing him until he ran out of options. Then they took him out."

"Maybe they were cartel enforcers."

"Cartel enforcers? Are you kidding?"

"No, dude! That shit was getting bad before the hurricane hit. With all the other stuff going on that was keeping the cops running in every direction, the cartels were fighting it out for territory, especially down in Miami and Fort Lauderdale. People did what they said because they were afraid of them, but the cartels provided protection from the gangs and other troublemakers too. They weren't out to hurt anyone that wasn't causing them problems or interfering with their business. But they are some seriously bad dudes, man. Get on their shit list and you turn up somewhere missing your head."

"Just like it's been in Mexico, huh?"

"Yeah, maybe worse. That shit was spreading all over south Florida. Probably all the other states along the Gulf coast too."

Eric knew he'd been away too long, but had no idea how bad things really were in his home state. He couldn't have talked Shauna into leaving whether they had stayed together or not though, so it did him little good to worry about her and Megan when it was out of his hands. Shauna loved everything about south Florida and Eric had too at one time. Growing up here with access to the water and all the adventure it offered had been instrumental in shaping the man he'd become. He was an excellent swimmer and expert diver long before he was old enough to join the Navy. He loved this state for many reasons, but it had always been too crowded, especially in the best parts this far south. He'd known even then that the population density was a liability in a disaster, as he'd seen the effects of that many times in the aftermath of lesser hurricanes. In a time of nationwide civil unrest and violence, it was inevitable that places like Florida would become truly dangerous. The only good thing about the hurricane was that its wake of destruction might hinder the bad elements as much as the good. Things were sure to keep going downhill though, no matter what, and Eric didn't have time to waste. He needed to get to his father's place fast and find out if Shauna and Megan were there or not, and try and talk his old man into leaving, whether they were or not. He told Jonathan what he planned to do, and how he was still weighing his options regarding the two water routes to his destination.

"Man, I don't know. That's a tough one! It's a lot farther if you go south, and you'll hit a lot of messed up urban areas on the way, but crossing the waterway, it's almost like you're gonna be trapped."

"I know, and I don't like it. Long stretches of canals and rivers would be a good place to run into an ambush, but so would parts of the ICW to the south. I could stay farther offshore going south, but if I commit to that I'm going to have some long hauls between stops."

"That's why you need to take me with you, dude, just like I suggested when we met. I can help paddle, and the two of us could get there faster than you could alone."

Eric wasn't as quick to rule out the possibility of taking Jonathan with him as he was before. The kid was self-sufficient and fairly knowledgeable when it came to survival, but beyond that, Eric had no idea. How would he react under fire if it came to that? He was untrained and had no combat experience, and Eric was certain that his own extensive skills would be put to the test before this was over. An extra paddler in the heavy two-man kayak would make a difference in his average speed though, and Jonathan seemed like he'd be able to pull his weight and do his part. Eric put off his answer for now. He needed to sleep for at least a few hours while it was daylight, and then he could make a better decision. Intermittent showers throughout the day kept the temperature in the woods bearable, and Eric slept soundly until he heard Jonathan calling him in an urgent, whispered voice.

"Eric! Wake up, man! There's somebody out there!"

Eric snapped to full alertness in a second, grabbing the M4 beside him as he rolled up to a crouch under the tarp.

"Where? How many?" he asked, scanning the thicket that surrounded them and seeing nothing.

"Out there, on the waterway. They're in a sailboat! They just dropped their anchor a few minutes ago, right in front of the little channel leading in here, of all places. I was fishing the mangroves just to the north when I saw them coming."

"Did they see you?"

"No, and I don't think they've seen your kayak yet either, the way you've got it covered up. But if they decide to come ashore...."

Jonathan went on to say that he'd seen at least two men on the boat, and that it looked like they intended to anchor there for the night. Even if they didn't come ashore and spot his kayak in the little channel, he would have to pass right by their boat when they left. That wouldn't present a problem if they were asleep, but if they weren't, he could be delayed for hours waiting.

"Stay here and I'll go see if I can tell what they're up to. Maybe if we're lucky they'll decide to move on before dark. It seems to me that it would be pretty stupid to anchor out there in the ICW in plain sight."

Eric worked his way down to the water's edge, staying low in the cover of the mangroves until he could see the boat through the foliage. Like Jonathan had said, it was a small sailboat with a cabin, maybe around twenty-five feet overall. There was obvious storm damage—bent lifeline stanchions and an ugly scar along the white fiberglass topsides just below the rail—but the rig appeared intact and there was a small outboard motor hanging from a retractable mount attached to the stern. Eric noted too that there was a dinghy trailing behind the boat, a small inflatable with plastic oars clipped to holders on the top of its main tubes. Whoever was aboard the sailboat might not have intentions of coming ashore, but the presence of the dinghy meant that they had the means to do so. Eric couldn't see the crew at all at the moment, as they were obviously down below in the cabin. What they did later would either be a serious problem or a minor inconvenience, but either way, Eric had no choice but to watch and wait.

Eight

"I TOLD YOU TO hang back and wait!" Eric whispered as Jonathan came crawling through the underbrush until he was beside him.

"I waited as long as I could, but dude, you've been down here more than an hour!"

It didn't seem that long to Eric, even though the evening twilight had faded to almost full darkness. He was focused on his observation and was unconcerned with the passing of time when in a situation like this. He had been watching long enough to ascertain that there were indeed at least two men aboard the sailboat, just as Jonathan had said. Whether there was anyone else aboard, Eric couldn't tell, but he'd watched the two come and go from down below to the cockpit several times. He'd also observed that both men were armed, one with a pistol on his belt at three o'clock and the other with a large revolver in a shoulder holster. Anybody moving about these days had good reason to be armed, but after what he'd seen the night before, it seemed plain stupid to anchor out there in a major waterway in plain sight. That was just asking for it. Judging from their appearance though, Eric figured these two had little to lose and probably just didn't care. They didn't look like the type of men who would have owned a sailboat in their prior lives either. It was pretty obvious they had found it somewhere or taken it from the real owner, and wherever they were headed they would likely continue taking what they wanted. Just a few minutes after Jonathan joined him, Eric saw one of the men pull the dinghy forward alongside the boat, so the other could step into it. Then he followed, standing in the inflatable and untying the line while his buddy readied the plastic oars.

"What do you think they're up to?" Jonathan asked.

"They're coming ashore, what else? Probably to go and look for something else to steal."

"They're going to see your kayak if they land on that sandbar. What are you gonna do?"

"Nothing yet. Just be quiet and watch."

Eric had been hoping the two men would stay put aboard their boat. He knew he might have to wait for hours, but they would probably go below to sleep eventually and then he could leave without them ever knowing he was there. Now they were complicating everything by heading straight to where his kayak was hidden. Just as Jonathan had speculated, they'd noticed the little channel winding into the mangroves and probably figured it would be a discreet place to land, just as Eric had when he'd arrived here in the dark that first morning. Even if the kayak weren't there for them to see when they came ashore, they would probably stumble across Jonathan's campsite on their way to the road. If Eric hadn't returned, this would be real trouble for the kid, considering these men were armed and he wasn't.

The two of them didn't stand a chance now, of course. Eric could easily take them out before they knew he was there if he wanted to, but he had to keep reminding himself he wasn't behind enemy lines. These men were probably up to no good, but they hadn't proven that yet and they *were* fellow Americans, after all. He would wait and see, and give them the benefit of the doubt and a chance to simply leave if they did indeed prove bad intent. He hoped that would be enough, but he was ready to do what was necessary if it came to that, and as they were now approaching the channel, it was time to find out.

"Wait here, Jonathan. I mean it this time. *Do not* follow me!" Eric whispered.

"What are you gonna do man?"

Eric didn't answer. He got to his feet and slipped through the mangroves adjacent to where his kayak was hidden, the M4 in hand and at ready as he watched the dinghy approach. The man at the oars was having a hard time keeping it going straight, not only because of the low quality of both the boat and oars, but also his obvious inexperience. The other man had a small flashlight that he flicked on intermittently, just enough to keep his buddy somewhat lined up in the channel. His reluctance to use the light more than necessary told Eric the man was aware of the dangers of being seen, and that this kind of nighttime shore excursion was nothing new to him. The oarsman banged his blades against the mangrove roots on either side of the channel as he attempted to stay in the middle, and Eric heard the other scold him in a low whisper for making so much noise.

He watched as the flashlight illuminated the sandbar once again, just before the bow of the inflatable touched. Then, just as he'd expected, the man swept his light along the bank and stopped when the beam found the black hull of the Klepper. The covering of branches he'd placed over it when he tied it up was never meant to hide it from close-up scrutiny such as this. It was enough to keep it from standing out to anyone traveling the waterway that happened to glance into the channel, but from ten feet away, the makeshift camouflage was far less effective.

"Hey, look at this!" the man with the light whispered.

"What is it, Tom?"

"Some kind of boat; I think it's a kayak. Look at these branches! Whoever left it here tried to hide it. That means they left and probably aren't coming back for a while. We ought to get it! It looks like it's big enough for two people."

"We can get it on the way back, after we see what else we can find."

"No, forget that! Let's just take it and go while the getting is good. Whoever left it here might already be on the way back. There's probably stuff inside it too. Let's tow it out to the boat and go anchor somewhere else where we can check it out."

When the man with the light began pulling the branches off of his kayak, looking for the lines securing it to the bank, Eric knew it was time to make his presence known. He still hoped he wouldn't have to kill these two, but since there were two of them and they were armed, he knew it was a possibility.

"That kayak belongs to me!" he said, causing the one with the light to stumble back in surprise before waving the beam in the direction of the woods, looking for the source of his voice. "Step away from it and get back in your dinghy and leave!" As he issued his command, Eric squeezed the pressure switch that activated his Surefire weapon light, putting a 300 lumens beam directly in the eyes of the man holding the flashlight. Temporarily blinded, the first man was no longer a threat, but Eric could see the other one stepping out of the dinghy into the knee-deep water. He was about to move the light to him when suddenly another beam of light from behind him lit up the second man, causing him to raise a hand to shield his eyes. Eric knew it was Jonathan's powerful flashlight, but he said nothing, as he was focused on the two strangers until he knew if they were going to comply.

At first, it seemed like they were. Eric swept the weapon light back and forth between them, ordering them to keep their hands where he could see them. But suddenly, the one in the water closest to his kayak turned to one side as if reaching for the dinghy, instead making a grab for the big revolver in his shoulder holster. Why he would make such a dumb move while at such a clear disadvantage, Eric couldn't fathom, but he swung the M4 into line with the man's chest and squeezed off two quick rounds. He would have let the other one live but even as his buddy was falling the second man was reaching for his own handgun. Truly they were men with nothing to lose, and just didn't seem to care. Eric took him out with a single round, and seeing that no follow-up shots were needed after sweeping his lights over the bodies where they fell in the shallow water, he shut off his light and told Jonathan to do the same.

"Damn, dude! You got 'em both before they knew what hit them! That was awesome!"

"They gave me no choice, unfortunately. But now I've gone and attracted no telling how much attention to our hideout with those three rifle shots."

"It may not matter. It just depends on whether or not there was anybody nearby on the road."

"Well, I don't intend to wait around and find out. If you want to come with me, go get your stuff together, and make it quick!"

"No shit? You're gonna let me go? Will my tent and everything fit in the kayak?"

"No, but it won't need to. We're going to *sail* to the Gulf Coast. It'll be faster and it will allow us to keep well away from the dangers alongshore."

Jonathan started rattling off questions but Eric hushed him with firm orders to get his ass in gear and make it quick. While he was off to collect what he wanted from his camp, Eric took the weapons off the dead men and then dragged the bodies away from the channel and into the tangle of mangrove roots where they would remain hidden in the shadows until daylight. Unless someone came quickly to investigate the sound of the gunfire, it was unlikely they would be found before the crabs and other sea creatures made quick work of their return to nature.

Eric had no use for the piece of junk inflatable the men had used as a dinghy, so he slashed the tubes with his knife and pulled it over the bodies as it quickly deflated. Before Jonathan returned, he worked to rearrange his gear under the decks of the kayak, making room for the kid to sit in the forward seat. There was a spare two-piece paddle stowed below as well, but Eric didn't bother with it now, as they only had a short distance to go out to the anchored boat. His decision to bring Jonathan along was made the instant he killed the two thieves. Their stolen sailboat was an opportunity that had fallen into his lap, and if it was seaworthy enough, as it appeared to be from where he'd studied it, the trip to the Caloosahatchee River was about to happen much quicker. Sailing around the tip of Florida offshore meant long hours at the helm though, with no opportunity to stop and sleep, so unlike in the kayak, Eric needed crew. Jonathan wanted to get out of here, so it was a mutually beneficial arrangement. Besides, the more he was around him, the more Eric liked the kid. He talked too much and he'd disobeyed Eric's orders to stay put, but in the end he'd been helpful by slipping up out of the dark and lighting up that second guy while Eric was focused on the first. Jonathan had a lot to learn, but Eric could tell that he was teachable, and more importantly, he had proven he had the balls to act in the face of danger.

When he returned to where Eric was waiting, Jonathan had his arms full of his possessions. The fishing rods and cast net were a top priority, and he also had his sleeping bag, machete and extra clothes.

"I left the tent, but I brought the tarp. Even though we've got the boat, you never know when we might have to make camp ashore somewhere."

"Good thinking. It'll work for shade when we're anchored too. It looks like the hurricane shredded the bimini top that was already on it. Come on, just get in and I'll paddle. You can just hold onto your stuff until we get out there."

"I hope nobody was following them from wherever they sailed from. It was pretty stupid to sail here in the daylight. At least it's dark again now."

"Yeah that's why we've got to make it quick and get the hell out to sea. We don't have far to go to get to the inlet, and once we get out to open water there'll be less chance of running into trouble, especially at night."

Eric said this to reassure Jonathan, but he didn't completely believe it. The truth was that a sailboat was much more visible than the kayak, even at night if someone hit the white sails with the beam of a powerful spotlight. And, if they were pursued by almost any kind of vessel with an engine there wouldn't be a chance in hell of getting away. But Eric was prepared to fight his way out of trouble, and deemed the risk acceptable because of all the days it would save him from paddling.

Jonathan grabbed hold of a lifeline stanchion on the starboard side of the sailboat when Eric drew the kayak alongside it. The metal manufacturer's plate mounted on the cockpit coaming proclaimed that the boat was a Catalina 25, just as Eric had thought when he first saw it. He had spent many summer afternoons as a teenager sailing with a friend who had a Catalina 22, a smaller sister to the 25. They were cheap production boats that could be spotted in practically every harbor in Florida, but they sailed well enough even if they weren't meant for offshore voyages. The faded vinyl lettering on the stern told him the little boat's name was *Gypsy*, much overused and unoriginal, but maybe that was a good thing now. Eric doubted anyone would be looking for it specifically by name anyway, unless the two thieves were being hunted by men like those from last night.

"It looks pretty rough, dude. What do you think?"

"I think it's perfect! We're not going to be entering any regattas. It's got a mast and sails and a working rudder; what more do you want?"

Nine

ERIC CLIMBED ABOARD THE sailboat with his M4 in hand and opened the hatch to clear the cabin before letting Jonathan board. There was no one down below, but the interior of the cabin was filthy, with dirty dishes piled in the tiny galley sink and on the table, and potato chip and pretzel crumbs smeared into the bunk upholstery and scattered all over the cabin sole. The interior also reeked with the odor of human waste coming from the small, enclosed head that was probably stopped up or overflowing. A quick scan of the lockers revealed that there were some unopened canned goods and gallon jugs of drinking water on board, but practically nothing in the way of safety or navigation gear, not even local charts. He hadn't expected much, since most owners of boats in that class used them for daysailing or racing, rather than cruising, but this one was bare bones. There wasn't even a working electrical system—no cabin lights, navigation lights, depth sounder or radio. But they didn't need any of that. He had his handheld with which to monitor the airwaves for marine traffic, and he certainly didn't intend to give away their position with nighttime running lights. Eric stayed below just long enough to inspect the bilges to make sure there weren't any serious leaks, and then climbed back out and waved Jonathan aboard.

"How is it, man?"

"It's filthy and it smells like shit, but it's a boat and it's not sinking. Come on aboard! We will pull the kayak up and lash it down on one of the side decks, but first I've got to get back in it and get the heavy stuff out. Stand right here and I'll pass stuff up to you. We need to hurry. I don't like sitting out here in the open with the anchor down, even if it *is* dark."

Eric dropped to his knees in the cockpit of the kayak and quickly opened up the heavy zippers that closed the fabric over the bow and stern decks. The boat was easy to unload that way, as most of his gear was packed into purpose-made elongated dry bags that fit well in the narrow storage compartments of the hull. Although he could have broken down the folding kayak itself and stowed it below deck in the sailboat, Eric didn't want to spend the time it would take to do that, and besides, he wanted the kayak ready at all times in case they had to abandon the larger boat for some reason.

"What in the hell have you got in these bags, dude? It feels like they're full of bricks!"

"The heavy stuff is ammo, spare weapons, magazines, explosives… most of the rest of it is food and water and assorted survival gear."

"I sure hope we don't get stopped by the Marine Patrol or the Coast Guard with all this shit!"

"Me too, but it's a chance we've got to take. What do you think would have happened just now if I hadn't had my rifle? Oh, and by the way, why don't you hang onto this? You might need it." Eric handed him the revolver in the shoulder holster the man who had tried to pull it on him had carried it in.

"Whoa, that's awesome, dude! A .357 Magnum? Hell yeah, that'll work!"

"It's definitely the better of the two. The .45 Auto the other guy was carrying is a cheap piece of junk."

"Thanks man! I feel a lot better about this situation already. Having a weapon gives a man a little piece of mind, you know?"

"Yes, I do know."

When most of the bags were out of the kayak, Eric resealed the decks and climbed back aboard the boat. Then he pulled it up over the rail by the bow until Jonathan could get ahold of it, and the two of them carried it forward, wedging it on its side between the lifeline stanchions and the cabin house. The curved decks of the Catalina 25 were far too short to accommodate the full length of the 17-foot kayak without the ends hanging overboard, but that didn't bother Eric because he didn't plan on coming alongside any docks.

As long as the jib sheets could run clear, that was all that mattered.

"How much sailing have you done, Jonathan?"

"None! I've spent plenty of time on motorboats, but I don't know shit about sailing."

"That's not a problem. You will by the time we get to Fort Myers. But since outboards are your thing, see if you can get that kicker on the stern started. We'll have to motor until we get through the cut."

Eric didn't like the idea of running the outboard in this relatively narrow waterway where it could be heard by anyone on the bank on either side, but they were in the lee of dense trees in the short section they had to follow north, and once they turned east for the exit at Jupiter Inlet, the east wind would be dead on the nose, leaving little choice. At least the little Honda four-stroke was relatively quiet though. Running it at half throttle, the sound wouldn't carry far. With Jonathan steering as he directed, Eric leaned against the cabin bulkhead and studied the passing shoreline with his night vision monocular, checking for movement, as they were within rifle range of land here. Despite the fact that the sailboat would be much easier to spot than his low kayak, Eric knew it presented a less-menacing profile. Anyone that saw the blacked-out kayak slipping in at night might assume the paddler was up to no good, whereas a sailboat could belong to an innocent family simply trying to get somewhere safe.

As they passed the park on the south side of the inlet, Eric spotted a man and woman among the shadows of the coconut palms there. They had seen the boat, as there was enough ambient light out on the open water that they couldn't miss it, and now they were standing rock still, thinking they were hidden in the dark. Studying them in the green night vision glow, Eric determined they weren't a threat, as they didn't appear armed and seemed only to be waiting for the boat to pass so they could get back to whatever they had been doing.

Unlike the morning he had first slipped ashore here, Eric and Jonathan were exiting the inlet on a falling tide. The ebb was helping them now, the current assisting as the small motor pushed the boat along, but once they reached the jetties; they faced a stretch of rough water they would have to punch through to get out. The Honda seemed to be running fine, but Eric didn't trust it completely, so with Jonathan steering and the sheets running free, he hoisted the main and then quickly unfurled the jib so as to be ready to sail the moment they had a bit of room to fall off the wind.

"Just keep it as close to the middle of the channel as you can, Jonathan, and give it some gas! Don't let the current turn us sideways!"

Eric studied the breaking waves they were facing through the monocular, judging their size. The wind was around fifteen knots this evening—nothing out of the ordinary—and he guessed the seas were running about four to six feet. He had little doubt that the Catalina could handle it, but she would take a pounding for a few minutes until they reached clear water beyond the breakers. He cleated off the main so it would be close-hauled as soon as they fell off the wind and then took the helm from Jonathan when they reached the worst of it. The jib was flogging, its slack sheets beating against the hull of the kayak and adding to the noise of the crashing waves, the darkness amplifying the effect and adding to the confusion. Eric could tell Jonathan was concerned, uncertain of what was about to happen.

"Nothing to it, man! The main thing is to take the waves at a bit of an angle to minimize the pounding, but not so much that she gets turned sideways."

"It's good thing we've got a motor dude! That's what I've never understood about sailboats; all of them have motors and most of the time you see them going places they're not even using the sails."

"We'll be using ours all right, just as soon as we get to open water. That five-gallon gas tank is almost full, but we need to save it for the Caloosahatchee River. You'll see the advantages of sailing by the time we get there."

"Maybe, but if we had my boat and enough gas we'd be getting there a whole lot faster."

Eric knew they were lucky the sailboat had any gas aboard at all, not to mention a reliable outboard and rigging and sails that were intact and functional. The hurricane damage it had suffered was mostly cosmetic; nothing that would matter for their voyage. The trashed interior was the result of two thieving slobs living in it with no regard to how it looked or smelled. Cleaning up down there was going to be a priority as soon as they were well offshore, because even if everything went as smoothly as possible, they were going to be aboard a few days, and they had to have a place out of the weather to sleep and prepare food.

Eric steered through a set of three consecutive waves, the bow crashing down into the trough behind each one with a shower of spray that soaked him and Jonathan in the cockpit. But the little boat rose out of the foam just like she was supposed to each time, shaking the water off her decks like a fighter shrugging off a punch, and never causing Eric a moment of concern. The channel widened as he drove her seaward, and falling off to the starboard tack, he was able to get some drive from the sails at last. Then she was close-hauled and reaching as close to the wind as possible, on an east-northeast heading that carried them past the last of the channel markers.

"See there, nothing to it, Jonathan! We'll stay on this tack just long enough to get clear of the coast, then come about and start heading south!"

"Are you planning on sailing all night?"

"You bet, and all day too! I want to get past Fort Lauderdale and Miami as quickly as possible, and I want to be as far out as we can be without bucking the Gulf Stream when we do it. So, we're going to need to set up watches; let's go with two-hour rotations since there are just two of us. It takes a day or so to get used to sleeping like that, but two hours is enough time to rest while off and not too long to keep sharp on duty. We'll sort it out and get started tomorrow though, because I know I won't sleep much tonight, and we'll need daylight to properly clean up that mess down below anyway."

"Those guys were some kind of nasty!" Jonathan said. "I might have been living in the woods all this time, but damn, at least I kept myself and my camp clean."

"I don't imagine they suddenly got that way because of this situation. I'm betting they were dirtbags before, too."

"You reckon they killed whoever owned this boat?"

"I doubt it, because whoever owned it probably wasn't aboard. It was just somebody's weekend toy and they probably found it washed up somewhere in the mangroves after the storm."

"I guess killing them and taking it makes us as bad or worse, doesn't it?"

"No. It wasn't theirs to begin with, although if they found it like that and the owners weren't around to claim it, then legally it might be considered salvage. None of that matters though, because the bottom line is that they were going to steal my kayak and they went for their guns. And don't forget, *you* tried to steal it from me too! The only reason I didn't shoot you the same way is because all you had was that dull machete and I knew you weren't going to use it."

"Yeah, that and the fact that you didn't have that rifle within reach. I guess I'd be a goner if you'd had it in hand. Man, was I ever stupid!"

"We learn from stupid mistakes if they don't kill us. I know I have. You'll have to learn those lessons a lot faster though, if you want to survive what we're dealing with now. There won't be time to second-guess yourself. It took me a while to figure it out and most people are probably the same. But now I do what has to be done, and when it's done, I forget about it. There's no room for thoughts of those dead men in my head anymore, other than cleaning up that shit they left in the cabin. You need to look at it the same way. Focus on what's got to be done now. No past. No future."

Even as he said it, Eric knew that was easier said than done. He was here in this situation now because of mistakes he'd made in the past, and he was hopeful of a future where he'd have a chance to make them right. Living in the moment was easier on the razor's edge of life and death, which was the thing that kept drawing him back, time after time, to combat. It was the down time in between the action that allowed thoughts of past regrets and future worries to creep inside, and now that they were beyond the breakers and sailing into the open Atlantic, Eric knew there would be long, tedious hours of nothing to do but think. At least until the next threat presented itself, which it always did, and most certainly would again.

Ten

Eric got the Catalina into her groove sailing south on a beam reach once they were approximately three miles off the coast—far enough to be hard to spot from land in the dark, but not far enough to encounter the northbound current of the Gulf Stream. Along this part of Florida's east coast, there was little to worry about hitting, even that close to shore. Like everything else on board that required power, the electronic depth gauge wasn't working, but Eric knew the waters out here were at least a couple hundred feet deep, and there were no reefs or obstructions. Because of this, he and Jonathan could focus all of their attention on the task of looking out for other unlit vessels, which was the real danger, whether from accidental collision or deliberate attack.

"This night vision stuff is badass!" Jonathan said, as he scanned the waters around them through 360 degrees.

"It's useful, but it's not foolproof. You've still got to use all your senses."

"Why don't you have one on your rifle? I thought you Special Forces guys all used those."

"It depends on the mission. It would just be in the way in the daytime, but that one can be mounted as an auxiliary to one of the M4s if I need it."

"One of them? You mean you've got more of those rifles? Are they full-auto too? Are you gonna let me use one? I can cover for you dude, I really can! I'm a pretty good shot even if I don't have military training."

Eric laughed. "There's one more, and you might get your chance; we'll see. Full-auto is not all that special though. It's not like in the movies where they just spray bullets and cut down all the bad guys. The regular M4s like this one have a three-round burst mode anyway, so it's not like they'll just dump the mag with one squeeze of the trigger. The other one I've got packed away is the M4A1 model that will though. It's useful for some things, but most of the time semi-auto mode gets the job done just fine, as you saw back there. Considering the situation we're in now, the last thing you want to do is waste ammo for no good reason."

"I hear you, but considering how heavy those bags of yours are, I figure you've got plenty."

"Plenty is relative. It goes fast in a hot firefight."

It was true that he was packing a heavy combat load, but what Eric hadn't told Jonathan was that all that weight wasn't just weapons and ammo. He was carrying something else that he knew might come in equally handy—something which could likely be used to purchase more of whatever he might need here if he could find the right people with whom to do business. When it came time to leave his lucrative employment as a security operator, Eric had accrued substantial earnings and bonuses, and he had negotiated for most of the balance to be paid in Krugerrand and other gold coins that would be more useful in the current economy than funds in some bank. The gold was heavy, but still compact and easy to carry and hide. Of course there was the risk of loss or theft, but to Eric, the risk was worth it. Once he found Shauna and Megan, there would be things they all needed, and implementing his plan to get them somewhere safer would require plenty of buying power. Eric trusted Jonathan well enough to let him have the revolver, and well enough to go to sleep with him on watch, but few were the men he had ever known that he would trust with the temptation of so much gold close at hand. Gold, like certain women and certain illegal substances, had a frightening power to make men do things they wouldn't otherwise consider. Jonathan might see some of the gold later, but there was no need for him to know about it now.

As they reached along in the dark, Eric taught him the fundamentals of sail trim and the feel of the helm. Jonathan was a quick enough learner, but steering a sailboat for the first time on a dark night at sea was disorienting for anyone. He overcompensated when the vessel rolled with the waves and inevitably luffed the sails more than once, but soon understood it well enough that Eric could leave him to it and attend to other matters. With his phone powered up again, Eric studied the satellite imagery he'd downloaded. He didn't have as much detail as he would have liked for their entire route, but combined with his memory of the region, it would be enough. Getting lost wasn't the problem, because following the coast as they were doing now was simple enough, even at night. Estimating progress made good and working out just when they would arrive at a given area was going to be a little more difficult though without the aid of GPS.

Eric could certainly navigate using a compass and dead reckoning, but he'd come to rely on the pinpoint accuracy of satellite fixes, especially when operating in unfamiliar territory at night. There were far fewer lights visible along this coast now than there would have normally been, and even though some of the lighted aids to navigation were still working, Eric couldn't identify them without detailed nautical charts. The best he could do was to keep an eye out for tall buildings, towers and other manmade structures they could see in order to guess which of the main urban areas they were passing. Eric would have preferred to slip by Miami-Fort Lauderdale in the dark, but at an average speed of only five knots, that wasn't going to happen. As the sky began to lighten with the gray of dawn, he edged the boat farther offshore to gain some distance from the dangers he was certain would be lurking there. The radio was on, the receiver scanning the full range of VHF marine frequencies, but it was as quiet here as it had been everywhere else on this coast.

Putting away the night vision monocular in exchange for his marine binoculars, Eric studied a line of commercial ships that were moored off the coast north of Fort Lauderdale, most of them approximately a mile offshore. He doubted they were waiting for port clearance as they would be in normal times, but for whatever reason they were sitting there stationary, and whether abandoned or still crewed he couldn't tell. A couple miles farther south, at the entrance channel to Port Everglades, Eric spotted a U.S. Navy destroyer. He wasn't surprised to see it guarding this once-busy port, and he had to assume there would be one near Miami as well.

"Do you think they'll come after us? Or just blow us out of the water when we go by?" Jonathan asked, when Eric handed him the binoculars so he could have a look.

"Not likely either. We'll pass by nearly three miles away from them. You can bet they would respond if we tried to approach much closer though."

"What do you think they're doing, just watching for terrorists or something?"

"Yep, standing by, ready for anything, I'm sure. I imagine resources are spread pretty thin by now, and only a few select ports and bases are under guard. It's logical they would still have assets here, as wide open to the world as this part of the coast is. They're watching us all right, but as long as we hold our course and stay clear, I think they'll leave us alone."

When they passed Government Cut at Miami, some 20 miles farther south, Eric saw that he'd been right when he assumed there'd be another Navy vessel posted off that major port as well. This one also was a destroyer, and like the one off Fort Lauderdale, it was anchored just outside the entrance to the ship channel. Jonathan was nervous as they passed it, but once again, the unseen crew aboard the menacing-looking ship was indifferent to the movement of a dinky little Catalina 25.

Eric and Jonathan had taken turns between the helm and keeping a sharp lookout with the binoculars as they passed these large urban areas of the coast. Once they were beyond the ship off Government Cut, it was time to begin the disgusting task of cleaning up down below. They'd both avoided even setting foot in the cabin throughout the night, but could put it off no longer.

"The holding tank is completely full and there's no overboard discharge, so there's no way to empty it," Eric said, after holding his breath and venturing into the head compartment. Jonathan knew little about boats larger than the outboard skiff that he'd owned before it got stolen, so Eric gave him the low-down on marine toilets.

"Like a lot of weekend boats, the head on this one was set up for dockside pump-out only, because of the legal issues of pumping overboard. It could be emptied with a portable bilge pump, but there doesn't seem to be one of those on board, unfortunately."

"So we've got to live with the smell, huh?"

"Yep, and with no way to empty the tank, the head is out of commission, so all business will have to be conducted over the side because there's not even a bucket on board. Still, I'm not going to complain. We're making good time and she's sailing just fine."

"Yeah, this isn't so bad. I thought it would be boring as shit going this slow, but I guess you're right; it beats paddling."

To Eric, the main advantage over the kayak aside from a little more speed was that the sailboat allowed them to stay far enough off the coast to avoid contact with people ashore. So far that had gone even better than he'd hoped, but it was inevitable that a confrontation would occur, and it did not long after the buildings of Miami dropped out of sight behind them to the north. Eric had set their course to stay just outside of the reefs and small keys that separated the Atlantic from Biscayne Bay, hoping to avoid any boat traffic that might be using the marked channel that ran up the middle of the bay, but that was not to be. Even though they were outside the reefs, they were still clearly visible from anyone using the channel. When a fast center-console powerboat appeared on the horizon to the southeast and suddenly changed course upon spotting them, Eric suspected there was going to be trouble. The boat was now heading for the closest cut through the reef that would take it out to open water where it could intercept them. Studying it through his binoculars, he was relieved at least that it didn't resemble the vessel in the canal behind Shauna's house.

"Keep it steady and just hold your course," he told Jonathan.

"Can you tell if they're cops or not?"

"I'm not sure yet, but I don't think so." Eric was looking for things like extra antennas, mounted blue lights or special markings, but the boat was nondescript, its finish the glossy white Gelcoat typical of nearly every other vessel of its type. He had been approached by official vessels in many places and situations over the years, including Homeland Security and Coast Guard patrols in these same Florida waters. Usually, the blue lights would already be flashing at this point if they were making an official stop. Or there would be a call on the radio, which there hadn't been. The lack of any such warning told him it would be wise to prepare for different intentions. To reach them here outside of the reefs, the boat was going to have to continue the other way, traveling for almost a half mile to the north before turning east through a channel entrance that Eric and Jonathan had already passed. That would give him a little more time to assess and get ready, but avoiding the faster boat all together wasn't an option.

"What do you think man?"

"I think this could be trouble, so I'm going to be ready in case I'm right. And if I'm not, then no big deal."

Eric dropped below into the cabin and opened his largest dry bag, digging through it to retrieve the fully automatic M4A1 that had the grenade launcher already attached. Then he draped a bandolier of high-explosive rounds for it over his shoulder and grabbed a handful of loaded 30-round mags before coming back on deck.

"Whoa, dude! Is that the other rifle you were talking about? Is that a freakin' grenade launcher on that thing?"

"Yes, it is. Just focus on the helm, man. You're heading up too much and luffing the jib."

"Sorry, I just wanted to see. How far can that thing shoot? Can you hit them from here with it?"

Eric laughed. "Not a chance. It's a grenade launcher, not a guided missile! Even when they get in range it would be hard to hit a moving target, but I imagine a 203 exploding off their bow might change their plans."

Before he took that measure, Eric wanted to give the crew of the boat the benefit of the doubt. He reached for the handheld radio, switching it to Channel 16 and called them repeatedly, asking their intentions and warning them to stand off. Each attempt was answered with only silence though, so

Eric put the radio aside, as it was apparent there would be no negotiation.

Eleven

ERIC KEPT HIS BINOCULARS trained on the powerboat as it reached the turnoff to the cut that would take it outside the reef. When it entered the open water outside, sure enough, it turned again, heading straight for them at top speed. As the boat rapidly closed the gap, Eric could see a man standing at the bow with a weapon in hand, and there was no longer any doubt of the crew's intentions. Eric didn't know what they expected to gain by attacking a small sailboat, but it was likely they expected little or no resistance. They were in for a big surprise though, and Eric was unconcerned as he loaded a round into the M203 launcher and estimated the range.

"Keep it steady, Jonathan. I'm going to send them a message."

Eric knew Jonathan wouldn't be able to resist watching no matter what he said. It didn't really matter if the boat veered off course a bit anyway, because Eric didn't expect to hit the approaching boat. He fired the round before the boat was within 500 yards, because he didn't want to give the man in the bow a chance to start shooting and he wanted to ensure the grenade traveled far enough to arm.

Much to his satisfaction, the projectile hit the water about 150 feet ahead of the speeding boat's bow. Eric knew there was always a chance of a dud when one of these rounds landed in water instead of hitting a hard surface, but this one detonated beautifully upon impact. The explosion wasn't huge, but the sudden eruption of spray it threw up was impressive enough to cause the driver of the boat to immediately veer off course. Whoever they were in that boat, they now knew that the crew of the much slower sailboat was by no means as defenseless as it appeared.

"That's awesome, man! They're lucky that one missed. Are you going to shoot another one?"

Eric had loaded another round into the launcher as soon as the first one was clear, but the boat had changed course to run at an angle off their port stern. Whether because they still intended to carry out their attack or he was simply venting frustration at being fired upon, the man in the bow opened fire at them with his rifle. Eric could hear the reports but there was nothing to indicate any near misses. Flipping the selector switch on the M4 to auto, he returned fire to dissuade the shooter, dumping a half-mag burst as he swept the rounds through the speeding boat from stern to bow at the waterline. This time the driver immediately did a U-turn and sped away to the north as fast as he had approached.

"You nailed them, man! That was totally badass!"

"Well, I guess if the grenade wasn't enough of a warning, they got the message now."

"That thing would have totally sunk their boat if it had hit them, wouldn't it?"

"Maybe, but that's not what it's intended for. It's more of a means to take out targets from behind cover. But there's no real cover on a boat like that anyway. Even the 5.56 rounds will go through the fiberglass like its not even there."

"Yeah, those stupid fuckers sure weren't expecting freakin' grenades and machine gun fire from a beat-up old sailboat! Dude, you taught them a lesson they'll never forget!"

"It worked this time, but keep in mind that every situation is different. That's why we've got to keep a sharp watch. This sailboat gets us out here away from most of the threats on land, but it leaves us exposed to anyone in a faster boat. If they had come at us with two or three boats working together instead of just one, it might have turned out a lot differently."

"That's why you need to let me have one of those rifles, man. With two of us shooting we'd have double the firepower!"

"It might come to that, but somebody's got to steer too. You're doing a good job of it, but I'll take it for a while if you're ready to get some sleep. We've got to get on our watch schedule, because it's going to be a whole lot harder to stay awake for a second night in a row if we don't sleep some today."

"Gotcha. I guess I *am* pretty tired. I'll see if I can crash for a couple hours if I can stand the smell down there, but wake me up if you see another boat."

"Don't worry about that. I can assure you I will, and you'd better have your ass on deck pronto when I do!"

"Yes sir! Whatever you say, Captain! I don't want to get on your bad side!"

"Then get some sleep! I'll wake you up at 1400 sharp."

Jonathan was obviously exhausted from staying awake all night and once he went below, he was quickly out. Eric was glad to have some time alone to think, as that had been nearly impossible with Jonathan's incessant chatter. When the opportunity to take this boat presented itself, Eric had instantly made the decision to invite the kid to join him. He didn't often second-guess his decisions, and he wasn't going to now. There were benefits and downsides to bringing him aboard. Right now, having crew to help him steer and keep watch outweighed any negatives. Whatever happened next, Eric figured he would worry about when the time came to do so. He'd always had a knack for making the best of questionable situations, and he didn't expect that to change now. Acquiring the boat at just the right time had been an extremely fortunate turn of events—at least for his immediate objective. But like everything else, there were trade-offs. The exposure to attacks like the one he'd just fended off was a perfect example that was not unexpected at all. He could choose that risk and get there faster, or spend three times as long sneaking along the coast in the kayak, trying to avoid detection. Either way, there would likely be encounters, any one of which could end his quest. Second-guessing his decision and worrying about the what-ifs wouldn't change that reality one bit, so Eric didn't let such thoughts intrude as he enjoyed these hours of solitude. Instead, he found himself reminiscing as he sailed along through these once familiar Florida waters.

Eric had spent a lot of time on and in the water as a teenager growing up in Florida. Diving was his first passion, and with easy access to warm, clear waters and reefs he'd quickly racked up hundreds of hours of bottom time long before he'd left home to join the Navy. The Keys offered the best diving this side of the Gulf Stream, so he'd spent a lot of time down here and had plenty of firsthand knowledge of the area. It seemed far too long since he'd visited that underwater world for the simple purpose of observing or perhaps collecting shells or spearfishing though. Underwater military operations were completely different—usually carried out in cold, dark waters with a single-minded focus on the objective. Even that kind of diving was relatively far in his past now though, as recent years found him working landlocked locations or on board ship with no need to get wet.

As the little Catalina 25 sliced through the clear aquamarine waters into Hawk Channel, Eric found himself staring wistfully through that window to another world thirty feet beneath the keel. Someday, he would return to those adventures of his youth that had so inspired and fulfilled him. When that might be, he had no idea, perhaps in the not too distant future, somewhere over the far horizon where he hoped to be after he found Megan. If she would just give him another chance, he would make up his shortcomings to her now, first by making sure she was safe, and then by showing her things and taking her places she would never see without him. It would be great if Shauna would go too, but Eric had few illusions about that. The best he could hope for was that he could also convince his old man to leave his boatyard and home. That was going to take some doing, but Eric was determined to give it his best shot. Life wasn't going to get any easier here in south Florida, and Bart Branson had to know that by now.

Whether his father would come with them or not, Eric knew he could count on the old man to help him find and prepare the right boat. They needed something far more substantial and seaworthy than this battered little Catalina, and Florida was the right place to find one regardless of the situation here now. Eric was willing to bet there would be a suitable vessel in Bart's own boatyard. He had the means to pay for anything within reason, although finding the owners to make the transaction might prove impossible. As he sat there at the helm, he thought back over some of the good boats he'd sailed in the past and figured something around 35 to 40 feet with a rugged full keel would do just nicely. Whatever he chose, it needed to be built to last and simple enough to repair in remote locations from locally available materials. Eric had a few choice landfalls in mind already—none of them the kinds of places where one could find a chandlery or other facilities on the waterfront. He was convinced that the best option for getting through this crisis and what would surely follow was to get someplace as far out of the way as possible. Ideally, that would be a place that was sparsely populated or uninhabited and one that others fleeing the war zones couldn't easily reach. He wasn't thinking of the stereotypical tropical island paradise most people with boats might consider. There was still plenty of coastal wilderness in the world if one didn't mind a harsher climate and the prospect of a dangerous passage to reach it. To live aboard in such places would require a simple, but solid sailing vessel equipped for long-term self-sufficiency off the grid. A hull of steel or aluminum would be best, and though good examples were harder to find than the far more common fiberglass, Eric had reason to believe his father would have a lead on just the right vessel. It might be hurricane-damaged and in need of work before leaving, but the thought of that didn't bother him at all.

The far bigger question was whether he would find Shauna and her family there at his father's place, and especially whether or not Megan might be with them. Eric really hoped she was, because if she was still in Colorado it was going to be a major expedition to get to her now and it would seriously delay his plans for getting out of the country ASAP. He remained hopeful despite his doubts however, and was so lost in his thoughts of fixing up the right boat and sailing away that he let Jonathan sleep well past the two-hour interval of his off-watch time. The kid finally woke on his own sometime by late afternoon, stretching and yawning as he climbed out on deck.

"What time is it, man? I was wiped out."

"Way past your watch! I thought I could count on you, but no, I guess I was wrong."

"I'm sorry, man! It's not really my fault. I thought you were gonna wake me up in two hours like you said. It's not like I had an alarm clock to set or anything!"

Eric laughed. "I'm just giving you shit, Jonathan. It's no problem. I would have woken you if I needed you. There's been nothing to report up here, and I've enjoyed the quiet time, to be honest."

"Sorry if I've been running my mouth too much. People tell me that I tend to do that, but damn, until you showed up at my camp, I hadn't spoken to *anyone* for weeks! Hiding out like that gets lonely as hell sometimes. Don't get me wrong; I can handle alone time just fine, but lately it's been a little much."

"Nah, it's okay. I don't mind the conversation or I wouldn't have brought you with me. But some time to think has been useful. I've been doing some planning while you were down there."

"Cool! I'd like to hear about it, but I'm leaving the decisions up to you, man. This sailing stuff is your world, not mine. Where are we right now anyway?" Jonathan asked, as he pointed to the distant land to the north.

"That's Key Largo you're looking at. We're in the outer edge of Hawk Channel, running just inside the reefs that separate it from the Florida Straits. We're far enough out to not attract attention from shore, but by staying inside the reefs, we've got smoother water. We'll run this southwesterly course we're on until we get past all of the Upper Keys. After Marathon, there's a long bridge with a high span way out in the middle. That'll be a good place to cross into the Gulf of Mexico when we turn north."

"I know the one you're talking about. That's the Seven Mile Bridge on the Overseas Highway. I've been over it going to Key West."

"Yep, that's the one. We can cut through there without having to pass close to any of the smaller keys and hopefully avoid any enemy contact."

"Like those fuckers on that speedboat, right?"

"Yeah, whoever they were. I say 'enemy' contact, but hell, I've got to keep reminding myself that this is *Florida*, and anybody we run into will almost certainly be fellow Americans. Sorry, but I'm just used to thinking in terms like that."

"I don't see anything wrong with it. Just because they're Americans doesn't mean they're not deranged and dangerous. Like I told you, they could be cartel enforcers or some kind of gang members. There's no way of knowing who's in control of these places we're passing by."

"No, you're absolutely right. In this kind of situation it's hard to know who is the enemy, but from what I've seen so far, we need to assume anyone we meet could be a threat. The dynamics of the threat will be changing as time goes on, too. That's the nature of insurgencies and revolutions. I've seen it in most of the places I've worked. It's the main reason jobs like mine even exist. Contractors can be sent in without all the politics and limitations that restrict official military ops. The rules are more bendable, and that's what makes it possible to get the job done in most cases."

"So they just send you guys in off the books to kill the bad guys and be done with it. That sounds smart to me. That's how the cartels do it too, from what I've heard."

"Killing is sometimes necessary, but we're not exactly hitmen, and not every operation is about a specific target. Sometimes it really is just security and we're there just in case a threat presents itself. In a case like that, you usually hope it does, because some of those assignments can be boring as hell otherwise."

"It sounds like a pretty cool job to me. I wish I could do it! I want to learn all about it. I want to hear some war stories, especially stuff like the most dangerous op you've ever been on, and what happened. I know they say soldiers don't like to talk about that stuff, but if you ever do, I'm all ears, man."

Eric laughed. "The most dangerous op? I don't know which one that would be, because it probably hasn't happened yet. It might be the one I'm on right now for all I know! In fact, from what I'm piecing together in the short time since I arrived back in the States, I'm starting to think it will be. That's why I want to minimize any contact with people here in the Keys and everywhere else along this coast as much as possible. I think we can do that by sticking to my plan, so that's why we're way out here. Like I said before, there's a shorter route to the Gulf through Florida Bay to the north of Key Largo, but we'd be setting ourselves up for an ambush winding through those mangrove channels. Besides that, with no detailed charts it'd be too easy to run aground there. This route keeps us in the clear. Once we are past Marathon and can see the channel under the Seven Mile Bridge, we'll turn north and cut through there, and once we're in the Gulf it'll be a straight shot north to Cape Sable and the Everglades. I guess you'll have a decision to make soon."

Twelve

ERIC THOUGHT THAT IF he were in Jonathan's shoes, intending to remain in Florida, he too might consider an Everglades hideout as a survival strategy. The kid had the fishing skills to pull it off, and he knew how to rough it, although the insect problem in that place would challenge even the toughest outdoorsman on an extended stay. If Jonathan wanted to go for it, Eric wasn't going to discourage him, and he would drop him off wherever he liked, but if he got off now, he'd be stuck there without a boat, same as before. Eric had already told him that there'd probably be a boat of some kind around his father's boatyard that he could take. The only issue was whether Jonathan wanted to risk going all the way there to find out, rather than simply bail out in the wilderness while he had the chance.

"Dude, I know the pros and cons either way. It's a tough call because I know I could probably hide deep in the 'glades and avoid any trouble. But I told you I would help you get over there to your dad's place, and I meant it. If I can get a fishing boat out of the deal, that'll be great, but even if I can't,

I'll probably be better off on the Caloosahatchee River than I was where you found me. The fishing's good everywhere in Florida, freshwater and salt; I'm not worried about that, so if you're not sick of the company, I'll stick with you."

"Cool. I'm glad to hear it, just as long as you're aware of the risks. I have no idea what we're going to run into trying to get up that river from the Gulf, but I *will* get there, whatever it takes."

"I don't doubt that for a minute. I don't know much about that area, but even if I did, it would all be different since the hurricane, although they probably didn't get hit as hard that far inland."

"No, but I'm sure it was hard enough to take out the grid and shut everything down. The whole area down at the mouth of the river that we have to go through to get up there is heavily built-up and crowded, especially Fort Myers. Getting through there might be dicey, depending on the damage level and how many people are still around. There's no use worrying about it until we're a lot closer though. Right now, the goal is to get into the Gulf. If this breeze holds we'll be even with that bridge later tonight, and we should have time to get under it and back into open water before dawn. By tomorrow afternoon, I want to be somewhere off the Everglades coast. If we can find a good hideaway there with no other boats, we'll drop the hook for the night and get a decent rest before the last leg of the passage."

"I'm wondering if there won't be a lot of other boaters already there with the same idea."

"It's possible. If so, we'll give them plenty of distance. I'd imagine the kind of folks that would be there now are the kind that are looking to avoid trouble, rather than cause it, but you never know. Anyway, if you can take it for a couple of hours, I'm going crash right here in the cockpit. You shouldn't have to mess with the sails, just keep a sharp lookout and hold her on about 210 degrees."

"No problem, dude. I've got it. Get all the sleep you need."

If he could indeed get what he needed, Eric would sleep for at least eight or nine hours, but that wasn't going to happen now. Even if they stopped in the Everglades to anchor he didn't plan to stay that long. Four or five hours would be a true luxury. Eric had trained himself to function on far less, however, and he set the stopwatch alarm on his watch for two hours before stretching out on the leeward cockpit seat with his head on a boat cushion.

When the urgent little chirps of the digital alarm snapped him out of it, Eric had slept soundly, rocked into deep dreams by the gentle motion of the sloop as it cut through the light chop of Hawk Channel. It was after sunset now, but not yet fully dark. Eric sat up and quickly scanned the horizon through 360 degrees.

"I haven't seen any boats, but I think that's the bridge we're looking for," Jonathan said, as he pointed to the northwest and handed Eric his binoculars.

Backlit by the last glow of light on the horizon, Eric spotted the elevated overpass that was without a doubt the span over Moser Channel, the pass they would take through the Seven Mile Bridge.

"Good job, Jonathan. We can change course now and run straight for it. We ought to be closing in on it in another hour and a half, so that's about perfect. It'll be good and dark by then."

After telling Jonathan the new heading and trimming the sails to a broad reach on the other tack, Eric leaned against the main cabin bulkhead and carefully studied the darkening horizon ahead, looking for vessel movement and lights of any kind on the water or the bridge span. But the whole scene was eerily deserted. There were no major ports here between Miami and Key West, so he hadn't expected to see Navy presence, but in normal times there would be plenty of pleasure craft plying Hawk Channel and coming in and out of nearby Boot Key Harbor at Marathon. It made sense that there would be little boat traffic after dark, but he hadn't spotted a sail all day. It wasn't likely that the hurricane was the reason, because this area was spared the worst of it by being on the weaker, western side of the storm's eye. Of course, residents here wouldn't have known for sure where it was going to strike, but many of the boat owners may have already gotten out long before due to the violence and subsequent economic meltdown. The Keys were close enough to Cuba, the Bahamas and the Yucatan that anyone with a sufficiently seaworthy boat had several options. But just because there wasn't visible boat traffic on the move didn't mean there weren't plenty of folks holed up in the many hidden harbors and anchorages spread throughout the scattered islands of the Keys. And there was always the possibility of encountering another fast powerboat like the one off Biscayne Bay. The grenade launcher had proven its worth that time and Eric was glad he'd brought it because getting caught in open water in a five-knot sailboat was a situation that could only be remedied by superior firepower. If it happened again, they might not be so lucky, so slipping through the Keys unnoticed in the dark was certainly preferable to the alternative.

"This kind of gives me the creeps," Jonathan said, as they closed in on the dark overpass looming above them, Eric at the helm and keeping the boat in the center of the marked channel.

"It won't take but a few minutes. Just help me keep a lookout and we should be fine."

Both of the M4's were close at hand in the cockpit. Before they were close enough for the sound of rifle shots to carry to shore, Eric had given Jonathan a quick checkout on the weapon. The kid might have exaggerated his experience some, but he hadn't been lying when he said he knew how to shoot. After he demonstrated that he understood the weapon's controls, Eric had allowed him to fire a few rounds on semi-automatic to get the feel of it. And he'd also tried out the .357 Magnum he'd given him. He hoped it wouldn't be necessary for Jonathan to use a weapon, but there was no point in having him aboard if he couldn't help out in a firefight. In a situation like this, there was simply no room for non-combatants, aboard a boat or anywhere else. They sailed under the tall bridge span without incident though, and with several hours of darkness to spare, were well away from the main chain of the Keys by daybreak.

"We're doing better than I expected," Eric said, when Jonathan woke from his two-hour off-watch nap in the cockpit.

"The wind is still holding, huh? I never would have figured we could go this far without running the motor some."

"Oh, I knew we could. There's almost always enough of a breeze in these latitudes. I know you said you always see sailboats motoring, and you're right, I do too, but that's more laziness or lack of skill than lack of wind. How do you think they did it before motors were invented?"

"I figured they got stuck a lot, sitting around drifting and hoping it would blow again."

"Sometimes, but not as often as you might think. Here, take the tiller a minute. I'm going to stand up on the cabin top and have a better look around now that it's light enough to see."

Eric made his way forward and stepped up onto the coach roof, leaning back against the base of the mast to steady himself as he studied the horizon with his binoculars. At first, he didn't see anything at all, but a second sweep through 360 degrees caused him to stop and focus on a point just off the starboard bow. It was barely visible even with seven-power magnification, but he could now see that it was definitely the silhouette of a sail. He didn't want to lose it until he could determine the vessel's heading, so he stayed locked in on it while he gave instructions to Jonathan.

"Fall off about five degrees to port so I can get a better view, Jonathan. We've got company up there almost dead ahead."

"Five degrees to port?"

"That'll be to your left. Just a slight angle, not much!"

"Okay, gotcha dude. Do you want me to load the grenade launcher?"

"Hell no! Don't touch it! That boat is miles away and it's just a sailboat. They may not be a threat at all. As soon as I determine their heading, I'm going to try and raise them on the VHF."

Because of the distance and slow speed of both *Gypsy* and the other sailing vessel, it was several more minutes before Eric was certain that the boat was southbound. It was coming their way, but not directly. His best guess was that the skipper was steering for Islamorada, rather than the pass at the Seven Mile Bridge. Eric watched it through the binoculars until he was sure they were close enough that the crew of the other boat would have spotted them. Then he joined Jonathan in the cockpit and turned the transmitter on his handheld VHF to the low power setting.

"I'm going to call them when we're within a mile of closing. I don't want to transmit on high power because I don't want anyone else to hear us talking."

"Sounds like good thinking to me, dude. I just hope whoever's on that boat isn't gonna try something stupid."

"I doubt it. A sailboat is not the best choice if you're planning to attack other vessels."

"Unless maybe the other vessels are sailboats too."

"Well if they're up to something, they're not going to like what they find here, so I'm not worried. Since they're obviously coming from somewhere north of here on the west coast, I think this might be a good opportunity to get some useful intel."

Eric studied the distant boat again through the binoculars before he keyed the transmitter to make the call. It was close enough now that he could tell it was a real cruising boat, probably around forty feet long. It was equipped with a dodger and bimini, and he could see rows of jerry cans for fuel and water lashed to the lifelines.

"Southbound sailing vessel in Florida Bay, this is the sailing vessel, Gypsy, passing off your starboard bow, over…"

When his call went unanswered, Eric repeated it word for word. This time the response came back immediately.

"Sailing vessel Gypsy, this is the Celestial Wind out of Bay St. Louis, where's your home port?"

Bay St. Louis! Eric was excited to hear this. If this boat had come all the way from Bay St. Louis, then they would know the status of things on the northern Gulf Coast, probably including Louisiana, where his brother lived. In the conversation that ensued he learned that they certainly did know, having weathered the storm in a protected bayou on the north shore of Lake Pontchartrain. Like Hurricane Katrina in 2005, this storm had re-strengthened in the Gulf and had made landfall with a devastating storm surge. Unlike Katrina though, it had come ashore well to the west of New Orleans, which meant Keith's AO must have been hit hard by the sustained winds as it tracked north over land. Eric didn't have to ask to know that the power grid would have been taken down across that entire region, certainly as far inland as Baton Rouge and probably much farther. Keith would have his hands full of trouble, but Eric was confident that he could handle it as well as anybody.

He hadn't known exactly what to say when the captain of the other vessel asked about his home port, so he just said North Palm Beach, since he had been there recently. The other man said that he had his family on board, including his in-laws, and that they were trying to get to the Keys and eventually the Bahamas. What he told Eric about the pass at Fort Myers and the entrance to the Caloosahatchee River wasn't exactly encouraging:

"We tried to get in there, because my first choice for going to the islands was to cut across using the Okeechobee Waterway. We weren't sure if the locks were still open or not, but figured it would be worth a try. But somebody has moored a line of barges all the way across the entrance to the channel at the mouth of the river. We couldn't tell if it was the local authorities or just the people still living there, but whoever it was, it was clear to us they don't want any boat traffic entering that river. We were afraid to get any closer, so we never found out what it was all about. We kept going down the coast instead, and that's why we're here now."

Eric thanked the man for the useful information and advised him to alter course and steer for Moser Channel, where he and Jonathan had come through. He told him of the speedboat attack and warned him not to risk the narrow channels north of Key Largo. Like many sailors with little offshore experience, Eric could tell this captain wanted to play it safe by sticking to protected waters and avoiding long crossings. That wasn't going to work now, as the real dangers were on land, rather than at sea. Hopefully, he would listen and keep his family safe, but other than pass on that advice, there was little Eric could do for him.

"So *that* sucks!" Jonathan said. "How are we going to get to your dad's boatyard if the channel is blocked? You think they'll let us through?"

"Who knows? But I don't plan on asking permission. Chances are, the answer would be no if they went to the trouble to barricade the channel in the first place."

"What are you gonna do then? There might be too many of them to fight, even with all the shit you've got."

Eric had to laugh at Jonathan once again. "Of course I'm not going to try and fight my way through. There's no telling who's in charge of that blockade. It could be gangs, law enforcement, or even military. There's a time to fight, but you choose your fights wisely if you want to win, and that situation doesn't sound like one that would be wise to challenge. We'll have to figure out a way to sneak around it, instead."

"Sneak around it? The dude just said the whole river is blocked. How can we sail around that?"

"Oh we won't be sailing. We'll have to ditch *Gypsy* when we get close. But that's okay. That's why I came in the kayak in the first place."

"Awesome! So we're gonna go in there like a couple of badass SEALs in the middle of the night right? Just like when you came ashore at my camp?"

"Something like that, yeah," Eric grinned.

Thirteen

ERIC COULDN'T HELP BUT be amused by Jonathan's enthusiasm. The kid was naive in many ways, but eager to learn and unafraid. Eric could tell he had potential, and he'd seen combat make men out of kids with far less. He had been only nineteen himself when he had entered BUD/S, and in recent years he'd been involved with training even younger combatants in several regions where military-aged males were a scarce commodity. He certainly didn't come here to the U.S. looking to get involved in the fighting, and the last thing he thought he'd be doing was taking a local that was a stranger under his wing, but it had somehow happened anyway, and here they were. Eric worked alone when he had to, but being part of a team was what he preferred, and for now he was glad for the company.

Jonathan had already proven himself useful, so Eric figured he might as well do what he could to make him more so. An extra set of eyes and ears couldn't hurt, not only out here aboard *Gypsy* on open water, but later on the upcoming trip up the river. Eric had come here to Florida expecting to reach his father's place by kayak anyway, so ditching this old sailboat that fell into his lap wouldn't bother him a bit. It was adequate for getting the two of them around to the Gulf Coast, but that was about the extent of its usefulness to him, especially now with the news they'd just gotten.

The prospect of a physical barricade on the waterway had occurred to him when he was considering crossing to the Caloosahatchee by way of Lake Okeechobee, but he hadn't expected there to be one at the river's mouth at Fort Myers. For whatever reason, someone must have gone to quite a bit of trouble to organize and man such a blockade, and he doubted passage would be granted for the asking. Eric wasn't discouraged, because he was confident he and Jonathan could get around it in the kayak. Doing so might involve portaging overland though, so that was another reason he didn't mind the trouble of bringing Jonathan along. Two people could carry the loaded kayak a short distance, saving the frustration of having to completely unload it and make multiple trips shuttling gear. Leaving the river later might prove more problematic, and Jonathan had already thought of that and brought it up.

"That's something to worry about when the time comes. Sure, I'll scope out the situation as well as I can on the way in so I'll know what I'm up against, but the important thing is getting in. That's the mission right now—to get to my father's place and find out if Megan and her mom are there."

"Yeah, I guess. But what are you gonna do if she doesn't want to go with you? You already said your old man isn't gonna want to leave."

"I'll talk her into it, and him too, probably. I don't see the appeal of staying here, but what do I know?"

"A lot of people I know didn't believe things would get as bad as they did. Before the storm, I mean. Maybe they think everything's gonna settle down and it'll be back like it was before."

"If they do, they're delusional. Sure, that would be nice, but I've already seen how this plays out in several other countries where it's happened. Yeah, things can settle down eventually, but not likely before they get even worse first. Whatever started this to begin with has got to be resolved somehow. One side or the other has got to get their way, to some extent, which means the opposition will have to give in to that same extent."

"From what I could tell, a lot of things started it. It seemed to me like people all over the country couldn't get along with each other anymore. They were divided about everything. Every time you turned on the news, back when there still *was* news, there were protests and riots everywhere, with people calling each other names and threatening to kill anyone that disagreed with them. I'm not very old, but I don't remember it being like that before, do you?"

"No, not at the level it's been for the last few years, but it's been brewing beneath the surface for a long time. I guess it's finally come to a head. People are easily led by the media feeding them lies to get them all riled up. Once they get to the breaking point, all it takes are the right triggers by the agitators to set off the downhill spiral into anarchy, which seems to be what has already happened. This has been building up under the surface since way before you were old enough to understand it; and probably even before I was. It's just the way things are when a nation finally gets to the breaking point with so many different special interests and too damned many people. Every great empire in the history of the world has fallen. Why should the U.S. be any different?"

"People think it's different. Or at least they used to. Lately it seems like a lot more people hate their own country than not."

"Yeah, well the ones that hate it do so because they've been taught to or because the media has been convincing them it's the right thing to do. My father used to always say it would come to this one day, but I didn't believe it would happen in his lifetime. I thought it would be a little farther out in the future."

"The problem is that without anything working, it's hard to know what's going on, or who is fighting who."

"Yep. That's pretty typical in these situations. That's why it's best to get the hell out, because you don't know who your enemy is. It's not like a conventional war against a common enemy or even a regular civil war. It's more what I'd describe as 'evolving chaos', so who knows when it will get better, if ever?"

"Well, I don't know how I'd get out. I guess I'll just find a place to hole up where the fishing's good like I did before and try to wait it out."

Eric didn't say anything, but he knew such a plan probably wasn't sustainable long-term. He would do his best to see that Jonathan got a boat of some kind, after they reached his father's boatyard, but beyond that, he couldn't really help him. While the kid seemed upbeat and optimistic now, Eric knew being alone with no family or friends would get to him eventually. Or worse, his luck would run out when it came to evading those who were desperate and willing to kill for what they needed.

They made landfall off Cape Sable by mid-afternoon, and Eric steered a roughly parallel course to the shore until sundown, which found them near the north end of the cape, where mile after mile of deserted beaches ended and the mangroves began. Although he could have pushed on, Eric knew it would be wise to drop the anchor for a few hours and get some solid rest. The going was about to get a lot harder once they reached the Fort Myers area, and this would be the last chance to stop before they disembarked from *Gypsy* and took to the kayak.

Jonathan was all too happy to stop as well, not because he was tired, but because he was dying to do some fishing here in the Everglades. Eric figured it was a good opportunity to acquaint him with the kayak and give him a few pointers on nighttime ops, so once the anchor was down the two of them offloaded the Klepper. They crossed the short distance to shore and then paddled into the mouth of a wide tidal creek winding through the mangroves to empty into the Gulf.

"You're going to have to be smoother than that," Eric told him, as Jonathan paddled with a choppy stroke that made little splashes with every dip of the paddle blades.

"I know, man. I'm just getting the feel of it."

"When we set out for real up that river, the slightest splash could get us killed."

"Gotcha, dude. Don't worry about me. I know how to be quiet."

Eric trusted that he would get it, and by the time they returned to the boat, he was satisfied that Jonathan could handle it. The kid had also proven his prowess as a fisherman once again, quickly hooking a couple of nice mangrove snappers for their dinner. The Catalina 25 didn't have much of a galley, but there was a portable propane grill designed to use in the cockpit, and Eric quickly got it going after finding a half-full disposable fuel bottle for it. Fresh fish was a welcome change from the dehydrated rations he carried in the kayak.

After estimating the distance to Fort Myers using the map images stored in his smartphone, Eric said they needed to be underway by 0300 in the morning. He planned to make the passage well offshore, keeping out of sight of land throughout the following daylight hours, and then arrive in the nearby area late the following night.

"That only gives us about five hours to sleep, but that's better than not stopping here at all. Try not to waste it. We can rotate watches through the day tomorrow while we're sailing, but tomorrow night is going to be a long one once we head for the river."

"So where are we going to get off the boat? Are we going to anchor somewhere like this and then paddle in from there?"

"No, we won't risk sailing in close enough to anchor. We'll just heave-to a couple miles of the coast and go from there. Wherever *Gypsy* ends up, when and if someone finds her, we'll be long gone. Now get some sleep! I'll show you the route I have in mind tomorrow. Nothing's set in stone though until we get there. There are just too many variables to waste time worrying about it now."

Eric woke to the alarm beeps from his watch ten minutes before he planned to get underway at 0300. He had never been addicted to caffeine so he had no use for long morning rituals of coffee drinking and other time wasters to start his day. He was used to sleeping in short intervals when necessary, and had trained himself to shut down and fall asleep the minute he hit the sack and likewise to wake up ready to rock and roll. Jonathan, on the other hand, slept through the barely-audible alarm and Eric didn't bother him as he hauled in the anchor himself and set the main and jib. As soon as Gypsy heeled over and began to make way, however, Jonathan was on deck, rubbing his eyes and yawning.

"Sorry man, I guess I was pretty wiped out."

"Don't worry about it. Sleep another two if you need it. Once we're in the kayak, there's not going to be anymore sleeping underway."

"I figured that. I still want to know how we're going to get around into the river though, if the whole entrance is blocked off and guarded."

"I'm betting that what they're trying to block is regular boat traffic. That doesn't apply to us in the Klepper. They'll have the navigable channel blocked, sure, but we only need six inches of water to float and we can pick up the kayak and carry it overland where we have to. Here, take a look at this:"

Eric powered up his smartphone and scrolled through his map images until he got to the one that showed the lower Caloosahatchee River. He wished he had a closer view, with more detail, but was grateful for what he did have considering the situation. He'd downloaded the view of that area only because he knew he would be going to his father's place at some point, whether he found Megan at home or not. He'd already studied the imagery he had, looking for possible ways around the reported blockade. None of the options were great. The Fort Myers area was heavily developed almost everywhere on the waterfront, but there was one intriguing possibility that might work.

"See that long point there on the south side of the river mouth? If those folks we talked to yesterday on the sailboat were able to see that the entrance was blocked from where they passed it, I'm betting that the barricade is located there, from the tip of that point to the closest adjacent point on the north shore. That's what I would do, if I were attempting to restrict boat traffic. It's as much a deterrent as anything else, because anyone approaching from either the north or the south can't miss it once they're inside of Sanibel Island," Eric pointed. "What I'm looking at is this dark area, farther south on the wider part of that point, where this little cove cuts in. It looks to me like that's either marsh or possibly mangroves, probably with plenty of small channels running part of the way into them. If we hit it in the middle of the night, we can probably paddle or drag the kayak across and enter the river again upstream of the barricade."

"It looks like we'll still be cutting pretty close to it. You think they'll have people guarding it at night?"

"We should assume so, yeah. We have no way of knowing who's behind this, and whether they are regular citizens, authorities of some kind, or thugs. The best bet is to avoid all contact with them. So yeah, we'll be close, but we'll have the advantage because they won't be expecting anyone to go around back like that. If we were as lucky as I was the night I came in, we'll have rain, but I don't see a cloud in the sky this morning, so I'm not counting on it."

"Well, it *is* south Florida, so it could change a half dozen times before we get there."

Eric knew he was right, but he wasn't going to bet on foul weather to help them out. Getting around the reported barricade was the first obstacle, but Eric knew they would have to be stealthy for the entire stretch of the Caloosahatchee. He hadn't been to the lower reaches of the river by boat in several years, but he knew it was a densely populated area, at least until farther upriver, where Bart's boatyard was located. The river blockade would be even more problematic when it came time to leave, if things went as planned and Eric could procure a proper vessel for the voyage he had in mind. That was too far out of the realm of the present to spend much time dwelling on it though. He focused on the horizon ahead and all around them as they sailed north, keeping an eye out for ships and other boats as they paralleled the coast far enough off to be just beyond sight of land.

Fourteen

ERIC GRADUALLY ADJUSTED HIS heading by mid-afternoon, when he calculated they were well past Cape Romano. By sunset he'd angled in close enough that the tall condominiums and hotels of Naples were clearly visible on the horizon. The southeast wind had held out all day and they were still making good time. If nothing changed, they'd be close enough to Fort Myers to launch the kayak in three or four hours. That would allow enough time to sneak in to shore and assess the situation, and if all was clear, make some distance upriver before daybreak. But just like when he'd arrived at Jupiter Inlet in the predawn darkness, Eric planned to be holed up in a secure hideaway before first light.

"It looks to be about 15 or 20 miles from the mouth of the river up to where we can expect the urban build-up to give way to countryside. You can add at least five miles to that from where we're going to get off."

"Dude, that's a long way to paddle in one night. Can we *do* that?"

"If paddling was all we had to do, sure. The Klepper's a slow barge, but we can still average about three and half miles an hour. Paddling is not the hard part though. First, we've got to get around that barricade."

Two more hours found them closing in on Sanibel Island, now dead ahead and visible on the horizon in the low ambient light from the stars and a quarter moon. The skies were still clear, so any chance of bad weather to conceal their approach was highly unlikely. That wasn't altogether a bad thing, however. This Gulf coast area was trickier at night than his landfall at Jupiter Inlet. Dangerous shoals and exposed sandbars were everywhere here, and even with GPS and electronic charts it was a challenging area to navigate without local knowledge. Eric was relying on all his senses now, listening for breakers and straining to see the outlines of buoys and channel markers as he steered towards the opening between Sanibel and the mainland.

Fort Myers Beach, two miles off to starboard, would normally be glittering with brightly lit buildings, but tonight there were only scattered clusters of dim light here and there, marking the locations of survivors lucky enough to have generators or solar-powered battery banks. Seeing these signs of life ashore, Eric decided it was time to heave-to and ready the kayak. With Jonathan's help, he lifted the hull over the lifelines and climbed into it to tie it off, and then began stuffing his gear into the bow and stern ends as Jonathan passed him the sealed dry bags. Getting everything situated was more of a challenge than when they'd unloaded it in the calm waters off Jonathan's campsite. The two to three foot chop was causing the sailboat to pitch and roll, the kayak slamming against it as Eric held it off with one hand while moving the gear with the other. When it was all finally situated, he had Jonathan pass him the two M4s, which he slid into the spaces on either side of his seat in the stern before sitting down to assemble the two take-apart paddles.

"Okay, you're all clear to board. Let's do this!"

Eric was paddling as soon as Jonathan was seated, wanting to get away from the sailboat before it damaged the kayak. With the jib aback, the main sheeted in to the centerline and the tiller lashed hard to leeward, the Catalina 25 couldn't sail, but would slowly drift away downwind until it eventually washed ashore. From where they got off, Eric was sure that wouldn't be anywhere nearby. The boat would likely pass to the south of Sanibel Island and end up in the open Gulf. It had served its purpose, but he was glad to be rid of it and happy to be back in the kayak. The motion was gentler in the Klepper despite its smaller size, as its lighter weight allowed it to give with the seas rather than resist them. By the time Eric got it moving at hull speed, Jonathan was beginning to help from the bow seat; trying to match Eric's rhythm and so they could synchronize their strokes.

"You can pass me one of those M4s whenever you like, dude. I probably should have one up here with me, since I'm in the front and all."

"They're good where they are right now, besides, you've got that revolver. Just focus on paddling! If we run into trouble way out here, which I doubt we will, we'll have time to get ready for it."

"Whatever. I just wanna do my part, you know?"

"Yeah, I know, so *paddle!* That's the part we've both gotta do right now."

As soon as the two of them were in sync with their strokes, Jonathan's efforts helped Eric maintain an easy cruising speed. Using the foot-controlled rudder pedals that were available only to the stern paddler, Eric was able to counteract the effects of the quartering seas and wind so they didn't have to waste energy with correction strokes. He was aiming the bow directly at the middle of the short causeway that connected Sanibel Island to the mainland, where a high overpass spanned the channel that led north into the Gulf Intracoastal Waterway and Pine Island Sound beyond. The river mouth would then be on the right, about two and a half miles to the north of the bridge crossing. Once they were beyond the span, he hoped to be able to evaluate the feasibility of his plan to get around the river blockade.

Eric was satisfied with their timing as they glided silently beneath a lower section of the bridge well outside the main channel. At just after 2200 hours, it was late enough that most people ashore would probably be settled in for the night, but still early enough to allow for problems and delays. He kept to the west side of the channel to maintain plenty of distance between them and a small marina just north of the bridge, but the docks and buildings behind them were dark and quiet. The shoreline just past it opened up into a small, dark cove dotted with mangrove islands. It was this area that had caught Eric's attention when he'd studied his maps and satellite images, as it was a pocket of undeveloped land in the middle of the long point that reached to the south side of the river mouth. If things were as they'd appeared here, he planned to cross this uninhabited area and enter the river upstream of the barricade.

"Just put your paddle down for a minute and let's drift," Eric whispered. They were in protected waters now, out of the wind, so it was a good place for him to stop and reconnoiter with the night vision monocular. Once they were in the shallow cove, he doubted they'd encounter any other boats, but remembering the shooting from the patrol boat in North Palm Beach, Eric knew they couldn't be too careful. From where they were entering the cove, they wouldn't be able to see the blockade that the man in the sailboat had reported, but Eric took him at his word that it was there. He didn't want to risk paddling farther north just to have a look, nor waste time backtracking here afterwards to get around it when they could just get started now.

"The canal network that I showed you on the satellite image earlier is on the other side of the point there, just north of this small cove," Eric pointed, before he started paddling again. "There's a creek that leads across into the development and it might be possible to paddle through it to the other side, but it would put us way too close to anyone that might be in the houses and boats that are probably there. We're going to have to do this the hard way and cross through the mangroves and marsh on this side of the development."

Eric knew it wouldn't be easy going, and probably not even possible if he were alone. Getting the loaded kayak through the clusters of mangrove roots wouldn't be feasible without unloading it first. With Jonathan's help though, that would go faster and he was sure the two of them could work it through one way or another.

When they reached the cove after crossing to the east side of the main channel, they soon found themselves in water so shallow that their paddle blades dug into the soft mud bottom with every stroke. Before they even reached the mangroves, they had to get out and drag the boat, sinking nearly knee-deep in the foul-smelling tidal muck with every step. It was brutally hard work and as soon as they reached the concealment of the trees, Eric whispered that they could take a short break. He looked at his watch. A full hour had passed since they'd passed under the bridge, and they hadn't even gotten to the hard part yet.

"That mud sucks, dude."

"Yeah, well dragging the boat through those mangroves is going to suck even more, but at least it doesn't look like they go very far. There's probably marsh and more mud on the other side though, and then there's the road going out to the point that we'll have to cross."

"What if we can't get through? We sure don't want to get halfway in the middle of this shit and have to turn around and go back to find another way!"

"Of course not. That's why you're going to stay here and guard the boat while I go have a look and check it out. No matter how long I'm gone; you wait here until I get back. Got it?"

"Sure, man. I'm cool."

"I'm leaving the other rifle in the boat," Eric said, as he picked up his M4. "Don't fuck with it!"

Eric was entrusting everything he had to the kid, but he felt confident he could do so now. If he was wrong, Jonathan could be long gone and impossible to find by the time he got back, but Eric often relied on his ability to read people and he had faith in his new temporary partner. He was also pretty sure that the kid realized the seriousness of what they were doing here and that he would indeed stay quiet. Eric didn't relish the idea of dragging the kayak into that thicket and back out again any more than Jonathan did, so it made sense to do some recon first. He wanted to get a look at the river on the other side of the point, and make sure they could indeed relaunch and paddle on in the direction of their destination once they were across.

Half wading and half clambering over root clusters, Eric wormed his way through the mangroves until he emerged in a grassy marsh, just as he'd expected. A huge splash in the black water ten feet ahead of him brought him to a momentary halt, but the startled gator wasn't a threat; it was simply trying to get out of his way. He hit a stretch of waist-deep water and then the swamp began to give way to higher ground as he approached the road. Crouching in the tall grass at the edge of the right-of-way, Eric paused to listen. He could hear the hum of generators just a short distance to the north, telling him that the point was surely occupied. The stretch of roadway that he could see was dark and deserted though, and satisfied that no one was around, Eric quickly sprinted across, stopping as soon as he reached the cover of the tall grass on the other side. There was more marsh and mangrove forest between him and the river, and it took a combination of wading, climbing and swimming to finally emerge on the northwest side of the point, where he at last had an unobstructed view of the broad Caloosahatchee.

Sweeping the shoreline with his monocular, Eric could see a cluster of commercial fishing vessels anchored in the river just north of the point. He couldn't quite see the river mouth from where he stood, but he was willing to bet that those boats were just inside the reported barricade. If so, it could be that local civilians had banded together to keep traffic out of the river. There was nothing obstructing the channel farther upstream that he could see, but here and there along both banks there were indicators of people in the form of generator-powered lights. The river itself was quiet though, deserted but for the group of anchored vessels. From where he stood, Eric felt it was possible to slip through the city and continue upstream in the kayak, but it had taken him another half hour just to push through to here from where he'd left Jonathan. It would take nearly as long to get back, and then probably twice as long again for the two of them to get the kayak and gear across without making undue noise. Eric didn't like it, but he figured it would be after 0200 before they were paddling again. That would leave only four hours of darkness to paddle upriver—not enough time to get out of the sprawling city lining its banks.

The other option was to move their stuff part way across and wait it out another day so they could get an earlier start. He didn't relish the idea of spending the night in such close proximity to so many people, but if that's what it came to, they would have to do it. The dangers of doing so were reinforced when he paused again before re-crossing the road. The glow of headlights to the south told him a vehicle was coming, so he backed deeper into the grass and crouched as he waited. The lifted four-wheel-drive pickup truck that passed him was crawling along at 10-15 miles per hour, but he couldn't see anything of the occupants through the dark tinted windows. Eric waited until it disappeared, and then he quickly crossed the road again and entered the marsh. If he and Jonathan were going to wait it out, the best place to do so was on this side of the road, probably in the middle of the mangroves between the cove and the marsh. It would make for a long day of sweating and slapping mosquitos, but it was better than being caught out in the open at dawn with nowhere to hide. He worked his way through the tangled roots until he reached the spot where he'd left Jonathan to give him the news, and much to his dismay found him gone! *The fucking kid was gone! And the son of a bitch had taken the kayak and all his gear with him!*

Fifteen

ERIC WAS SO FURIOUS he could have torn the kid's head off with his bare hands, but he was even more furious with himself. How could he have been such an idiot after Jonathan already tried to steal his kayak once? He'd let down his guard and trusted him completely, and now he'd lost everything—stranded in a mangrove swamp with no boat and nothing but his rifle. He waded out into the edge of the water and stood there shaking with rage as he scanned the shadows along the shores of the cove with the monocular. If he could just catch of a glimpse of him slipping away, he would dump a full mag into his sorry ass even if it did bring every son of a bitch on the point running this way to investigate. But he'd been gone more than an hour. If Jonathan left shortly after he did, Eric knew he wouldn't be anywhere near the little cove now. Eric stood there seething; wanting to scream out loud as he wondered what in the hell he was going to do now. Finding another boat was about his only option, but nothing would replace all he'd lost in that kayak—especially the gold—without which he had nothing to even trade for one. He was about to turn back into the mangroves to cross the point again and figure it out when suddenly; a beam of light hitting the treetops to the south caught his eye.

The light swept through the mangroves and out across the water, but he couldn't see the source as it was coming from somewhere in one of the little dead-end channels that wound into the trees from the cove. Eric knew it wasn't Jonathan, because there wasn't a spotlight that bright in the kayak. This one appeared to be a 12-volt Halogen spotlight, the kind many people carried aboard their boats for lighting up channel markers and such. The light flicked on and off a couple of times, and though Eric listened, he heard no sound of a motor. He began making his way quietly through the trees in the direction of the light, stopping here and there to peer out into the dark bay with the night vision monocular. Finally, he saw the source of the light. A dark hull glided silently out of the mangroves, and he could see the silhouette of a standing man on the elevated platform at the stern. It was a flats fishing boat, running an electric trolling motor, hence the reason he'd heard no sound. In the green glow of the monocular, Eric could now see that the man held a bowfishing rig in his hand, and that a portable spotlight was mounted on the low pulpit beside him. The man was hunting the mangrove channels, evidently shining the clear water, looking for targets for his barbed arrow. Eric watched as he slowly worked his way along the shore to the south, checking each opening in the mangroves as he gradually headed towards the exit from the cove. *Had he already fished this spot where Eric had left Jonathan? Did this somehow explain the kid's absence?* Eric got his answer five minutes later, when the lone boatman finally disappeared around the point to the south. A single whippoorwill call emanated from somewhere in the dark mangroves to the north. At first it was a single, solitary whistle. Then after nearly a full minute of quiet, while Eric tried to decide whether or not it was real, the call resumed, over and over with sudden urgency. Eric answered back with one of his own.

"You son of a bitch!" Eric whispered, as Jonathan paddled out of the shadows from the north and glided towards the bank in his kayak. "I was ready to shoot you on sight!"

"That was a close call, dude! I saw that guy come into the cove right after you left. I saw what he was doing, going up into every little channel his boat could fit in, looking for snook or whatever, and I knew if I stayed here he would see me. I got in the kayak before he got close enough, and I was lucky there was a tiny little creek about a hundred feet up that way that's only about three feet wide. I got out and pulled the kayak up in there as far as I could get it, and then I just settled down and watched. That dude came right by here, man! He saw the channel I was in, but he couldn't get in there. I watched him for a good thirty minutes, and didn't think he would ever leave, until he finally turned around and headed back the way he came. I was ready though. I had the M4 you left ready to light up his ass if he saw me and started shooting or something. You didn't really think I'd cut out on you, did you man?"

Eric just shook his head and turned away as Jonathan stepped out of the kayak and pulled it up in the mud beside him. Yeah, he really did think that at the time, and yeah, he'd been furious enough to kill. It wouldn't have been the first time he'd been betrayed if it had happened, but he didn't say anything else about it. He just told Jonathan what he'd found on his recon of the point, and how he was thinking about waiting it out until the following night. That option was looking even better now, as they'd just lost another half hour to this little fiasco.

The two of them unloaded the kayak and carried it through the mangroves to the edge of the marsh that separated them from the road. Once they had all the gear there too, they pitched Jonathan's camouflaged tarp well within the tree line and settled in to wait, first for morning and then for the end of the long coming day.

"I hate to waste the rest of the night and all day tomorrow sitting here like this, but even if we could put into the river on the other side right now, I doubt we'd get past all of the city before daylight. Finding a good hideout up there might be iffy, especially one as good as this."

"I'm cool with it man. I can slip back through there to the edge of the cove later and do some fishing. It's not like I've got anywhere I've got to be tomorrow."

Eric envied the kid in a way. With no family and no one to be responsible for other than himself, he was truly free. Eric had wanted to be that way too when he was that age, but the pull of adventure and danger was too strong, and he'd signed away his freedom when he enlisted. At the time, he'd considered it a fair trade. He would follow orders and become the property of the U.S. Navy in exchange for the toughest and best training available on the planet. Eric was as gung-ho as they came when he made the cut and earned his place on the team, and that enthusiasm had stayed with him and sustained him through times and experiences that would have broken lesser men.

He had made it out alive when many of his buddies did not. Eric would have gladly traded places with any one of them if it were possible, but apparently it wasn't his destiny to die in service to his country. He didn't regret the trade off, giving up his youth and personal freedom to try and make a difference, but he knew now he'd gone too far in the end. He had done his time long ago and like Shauna kept telling him, it should have been enough. If he had listened, he might still have a family, and he probably wouldn't be wondering whether he'd find his daughter up that dark river ahead of them or if she was still some 2,000 miles away in Colorado.

Eric and Jonathan took turns standing watch throughout the following day. They heard the occasional vehicle passing on the nearby road and a few motorboats running up and down the channel, but there was little danger of anyone wandering into the heart of a mangrove swamp without good reason. Mosquitos and deer flies, combined with the Florida heat and humidity made the day drag on, as there wasn't nearly as much of a breeze reaching the woods here as there had been at Jonathan's east coast camp. When night finally rolled around again, the two of them wasted no time getting moving. Eric wanted to have the kayak and all the gear in position on the other side as early as possible.

"I figure if we wait until about 2100 hours, we should be good to go," he told Jonathan, as they sat on the riverbank, watching an occasional runabout go up or down the channel.

"I guess there's always the chance of running into a fisherman like that dude bowfishing last night," Jonathan said.

"Yeah well, we can't wait forever. We'll have to take our chances with that. Just because someone sees us, it doesn't automatically mean there'll be a problem. Every situation is different. Just back me up with another set of eyes and ears, and remember, don't splash that damned paddle!"

They favored the south shore as much as possible for the first couple of miles, trying to keep out of the line of sight of anyone that might be manning the barricade at the mouth of the river. When they had traveled a sufficient distance from their start point, Eric could see that the barricade was indeed there. It appeared to be just as the man from the sailboat described it—a raft of moored steel barges, completely blocking the entrance to and exit from the river. The small boats they'd heard running up and down the channel from the outside were probably cutting through the canals that accessed the waterfront development near the end of the point. Either that, or whoever was in charge had a narrow opening in the barricade to admit such smaller craft. One thing was certain; getting back out to the Gulf from upriver in a larger craft was going to mean getting past that barricade. Whether that was possible through negotiation, Eric didn't know, but it was indeed going to be a problem later on when the time came to deal with it.

Two miles upstream, the river narrowed as they passed Cape Coral on the north side. Eric and Jonathan spotted a man quietly paddling downriver in a dark green canoe, trying to keep to the shadows the same as them. Eric was sure the man must have seen them in the kayak, but if he had, he did nothing to indicate it. Whether he was a local resident simply using his canoe for transportation or a thief sneaking quietly along the waterfront, they had no way of knowing. Surely other survivors here were using canoes and kayaks for transportation, given the popularity of recreational paddling in these waters before. Even if the lone paddler wasn't a threat though, Eric didn't like being seen. The scenario that played out before his eyes in front of Shauna's dock was a vivid reminder of the importance of stealth, and he just wanted to get out of this city and upstream to the more remote parts of the river as quickly and quietly as possible.

There were several bridges they had to pass under above Cape Coral, and each time they approached one, Eric whispered to Jonathan to stop paddling so he could examine it with the night vision. But as they continued upriver, the bridges were fewer and farther apart, until at last they crossed under the twin spans of Interstate 75 where the river narrowed significantly. Here there were small, wooded islands outside of the main channel, as well as side creeks winding back into dense forests. A short distance upriver from the interstate, Eric spotted one such island too good to pass up. It was less than two hours until daylight again, so they pulled the kayak into the dense vegetation and made another day camp to wait for night to return. It was hard waiting when they were so close, but Eric refused to travel the river in the daylight.

"So, you're sure we'll make it all the way there tonight?" Jonathan asked, when the setting sun finally marked the end of another long day of waiting.

"Yep. I know this part of the river well. It's about 20 miles to La Belle, but my father's place is on this side of there, maybe 17 or 18 miles from here, tops."

"He's sure going to be surprised when you show up, I'll bet."

"I have no doubt of it. I'm sure he knows I would come back to the States looking for Megan, but still, he won't be expecting me, especially not arriving in a kayak. We're going to have to be careful paddling up there though. Hell, my old man is probably more likely to shoot us than anybody we've seen yet, and you can bet that he won't miss! I damned sure don't wanna go sneaking up to the dock behind his house in the dark. That would just be asking for it."

"So what are we gonna do? Wait for daylight to go see him?"

"Yep. We'll stop at his boatyard. It's a little ways downriver from his house, maybe half a mile. I figure we'll pull in there and just wait. I imagine he'll be down there to check on things come first light anyway. He's not one to sit still for long, and knowing him like I do, he's probably still working on boats every day even though the owners may never come back to pay him."

"He sounds like quite the character. I can't wait to meet him."

"He may give you a hard time at first, but just let me do the talking and it'll work out okay. We'll get you set up with a boat, I'm sure of it."

Jonathan said he didn't doubt that, but he wondered if he even needed one if he stayed around here. They'd already seen the dangers of traveling by water, and with the barricade downriver and what Eric had witnessed in North Palm Beach, it might be wiser to stay off the waterways. Eric couldn't argue with what he was saying. Jonathan's prospects here were dicey despite his excellent fishing and camping skills. They would talk about all that again later though. Right now Eric needed his help to paddle. He was growing more anxious by the mile, knowing that come morning, he would have his answers. Megan would either be at his father's house or she would not.

Sixteen

BART BRANSON SCANNED THE waters of the harbor between his position and the far end of the dock, waiting for the two fishing kayaks to reappear. He'd spotted them in the moonlight as they approached from across the river, using the docks for concealment as they closed on the shoreline that fronted his boatyard. If they landed, which was what he fully expected them to do, the paddlers would be in view as soon as they stepped ashore. Considering the hour and the stealthy nature of their approach, Bart had little doubt of their intentions.

With his Springfield M1-A steadied on the steel bulwark at the bow of a commercial fishing trawler blocked up on the hard on the west side of the property, Bart swept the reticle of his low-light scope across the black waters of the harbor. He couldn't pick out all the details in the shadows, but he was mainly looking for movement, checking to be sure there weren't more than the two he already knew were there. Kayaks were a first since he'd taken to keeping nighttime watches over the yard, but Bart wasn't really surprised to see them. Fishing from small sit-on-top kayaks had exploded in popularity in recent years, and plenty of the inexpensive plastic boats were still around, adapted to every purpose by those lacking better options in hard times. Bart had to admit that these two characters, whoever they were, seemed smarter than those he'd already dispatched. The kayaks were an excellent idea really, and a 2 a.m. raid conducted from small, silent watercraft certainly put the odds of success in their favor—or at least should have. But what these would-be-looters didn't know was that their predecessors had already set them up for an untimely demise. When his yard manager and another worker who'd been with him for years were murdered just weeks before, Bart had made up his mind to take matters into his own hands. In the absence of effective law enforcement, there was little else he *could* do.

Bart knew people had to survive, but raiding his boatyard in the middle of the night wasn't going to improve their odds of doing so. People were desperate, and the enormity of the situation turned even good folks to deeds they wouldn't have considered before, but sorting out the good from the bad while they were in the act wasn't something Bart was equipped to do. As far as he was concerned, anyone taking advantage of other folk's misfortune in times of disaster deserved no mercy, and none would be given, at least not by him.

The two paddlers landed exactly where he expected they would. There was a narrow beach on the side of the dock opposite the Travelift slipway, and it was the logical place to land small boats. He focused on the lead paddler, who stepped ashore and quickly pulled his boat up onto the strip of grass above the beach. The second kayaker landed in the same place and when both boats were secured, the two men bent over them to retrieve their weapons and tools.

Bart didn't have to guess what they were after. The bolt cutters and heavy pry bar one of the men carried told him all he needed to know. They were slipping into the dark boatyard with the intention of taking anything useful that they could strap to the decks of their kayaks. Most of the yachts and working vessels on the hard there still contained stores of fuel, liquor, food and other commodities, as well as valuables like electronics and systems components. Several of them had already been hit while Bart was away, most of those the night that his two employees were killed, but he was determined it wasn't going to happen again.

The man with the tools followed closely behind the one in the lead, who was carrying a pump-action shotgun at the ready as he picked a route into the yard that kept them within the shadows. The second man had a weapon slung over his shoulder as well, but he was relying on his buddy as they made their advance. Bart watched and waited, taking his time. Their intentions were clear enough that he had no qualms about taking them out before they even touched one of the boats, but there was no rush. Well hidden 15 feet above them on the deck of the dry-docked trawler, there was little chance the two men would suspect they were already in the crosshairs of the yard owner's riflescope. He would wait until they boarded one of the vessels, and then document the evidence with photos of the bodies along with their weapons and tools. Bart doubted he'd ever need it, but he liked documentation. It was a simple enough extra step that in his opinion it was worth the minor inconvenience, no matter how unlikely it was that anything that happened here would ever be questioned. It wasn't like the situation was going to suddenly get better, although Bart knew that plenty of people were still in denial about that.

South Florida wasn't the best place to be right now; especially in the aftermath of a hurricane that added to the misery and suffering that had begun months before it struck. Despite all that though, Bart was a lot better off than most folks here. Considering all the stores aboard the vessels in his yard, he had everything he needed for the foreseeable future. If worse came to worse and life became impossible here, he had his choice of seaworthy vessels in which to set sail for other shores. The boatyard was out in the boonies away from the urban sprawl near the coast, but still connected to the waters of the world, situated as it was on the banks of a navigable river. Bart doubted there were many places in the

U.S. where he'd be any better off, and if there were, they were in the remote mountain and desert areas that he had no means to reach anyway. The whole country had simply gone to hell in short order, and at this point a hurricane wasn't nearly the worst thing that had happened.

The two thieves made their way straight to the stern of a 54-foot Viking Convertible sport fisherman that Bart had hauled months before. The yacht was blocked up and the bottom had been cleaned and sanded for fresh paint right before Bart lost his maintenance crew and work was shut down. Like most of the vessels in his yard, it was likely to remain where it sat for a long time, if not indefinitely. Bart hadn't heard a word from the owner over the entire summer and had no idea where he was, or even if he was still alive. With the whole economy already flushed down the toilet and insurance companies nowhere in sight, most such playthings of the formerly wealthy would remain abandoned where they were left. But they were still private property, and according the service contracts signed by their owners, they were Bart's property until the yard bills were paid.

Bart had little personal interest in vessels like the Viking though, as it was far too fuel-thirsty to be useful in any practical way in this reality. A luxury sport fishing vessel was the last thing anyone needed right about now, but there were useful things on board, and the two men from the kayaks could barely make a dent in it all even if Bart wasn't there to put a stop to their pilfering. That was beside the point, though. Whether they took one item or stripped it bare they were looting on his property, and Bart intended to make sure they didn't get away with it.

He watched and waited while the two found a yard ladder and propped it up against the stern swim platform so they could climb aboard. The time to shoot was coming, and he adjusted his position to allow more relaxed breathing, sweeping the scope across the cockpit above the men to assess the best spot to cut them down before they broke inside. Even though it wouldn't matter in the grand scheme of things, he wanted to avoid putting a round through the topsides or the expensive glass salon doors. The Viking might never float again, but that was still no excuse for shooting up a 1.2 million dollar yacht. With that in mind, Bart decided the time to act was the moment the first man stepped off the ladder onto the platform. That would eliminate the possibility of him trying to hide behind the waist-high cockpit coamings, and if he didn't fall off when he died, the body would be easier to shove overboard to the ground. The second man would likely still be on the ladder or on the ground, but there was little cover close at hand even if he realized what was happening before it was his turn too.

Bart locked in on the first one and watched him climb the ladder. There was enough ambient light to center the reticle, but not enough to see all the details. He had seen just enough of them to know that both of the intruders were white males, and from the easy way they moved, probably young and fit. It was likely that both of them had prior experience with this sort of thing, probably even before the insurrection. There had never been a shortage of criminals in south Florida, but they surely had more competition these days than ever before.

Bart's finger was resting lightly on the trigger as he tracked his target to the top of the ladder. The range was close; less than 40 meters, and with the rifle resting on the trawler's bulwarks, a botched shot was highly unlikely. The man stepped off the ladder as soon as he was even with the swim platform, and just as Bart hoped he would, he stood there for a moment, studying the yacht from his new perspective while his partner mounted the ladder to follow him. Bart centered the crosshairs on the man's temple and squeezed the trigger, sending the match-grade 168-grain .308 round downrange. He saw the target immediately disappear from his field of view in the scope and he quickly swept it down to acquire the second one.

The other man's reaction was faster than he expected. Whether he saw his partner's head disintegrate first or heard the rifle blast, Bart wasn't sure, but he leapt away from the ladder and dove to the ground, crawling as fast as he could in the direction of the blocked-up keel. There was no way he could have pinpointed where the shot came from, but he was keeping low on instinct, heading for the nearest solid cover in the vicinity. It was simply too far in the end though, and he never had a chance. Bart opened up on him with four rapid-fire rounds, sweeping his aim through the man's line of travel from his legs to his head. He saw his target collapse, the body twitching for a few seconds more and then all was quiet and still again, as if nothing at all had happened.

Bart watched and waited for several more minutes, scanning the shoreline and the waters of the river once more for any sign of accomplices, but nothing else moved out there. He knew the sound of his rifle shots would have carried a great distance in the still of the night, but if anyone heard them, it was unlikely they would come looking for the source, especially at this hour. Bart stood and made his way aft to the stern of the trawler and descended the ladder to the ground. He would get his photos and secure the dead men's weapons and kayaks first, and when daylight came, he would dispose of the bodies just as he'd done the last time this happened.

Seventeen

BART QUIETLY MADE HIS way over to the Viking 54 where the two would-be looters were sprawled lifeless on the gravel. The first one he'd shot had been carrying a Mossberg 590 12-gauge pump shotgun—a decent close quarters weapon that Bart would gladly add to his growing arsenal. The second man who had tried to crawl for cover never had time to remove his shouldered rifle, which Bart could now see was a Chinese SKS. It wouldn't be the first one of those he'd taken off the body of a slain foe, but the last time that happened it was in a remote village near the border of Cambodia. Back then he'd been forced to trust his life to the M-16 he'd been issued, but Bart had never liked the Stoner design or the caliber. The .308 he'd used tonight did a better job in every way, and it didn't matter if the rifle and ammo weighed more, because Bart's days of humping his gear through the jungle were over—or at least he surely hoped so. He knew his two sons were comfortable with the modern M4 platform derived from that rifle he'd grown to hate, but they'd failed to convince him to give up his Springfield. Bart wondered about his boys on nights like this, but he knew they could take care of themselves. He'd given them the training and attitude early on that they needed to succeed in life, and both had chosen their professions fully understanding the risks, which were greater today than ever before. Bart didn't know when he'd see them again, especially Eric, but he knew they'd both approve of their old man tonight. Bart might be a long way from his prime at 69 years old, but he could damned well hold his own and both of those boys knew it.

He powered up his little Sony digital camera and snapped the photos he felt that he needed, making sure to include the weapons next to the bodies. The built-in flash illuminated them well enough even in the dark, but there wasn't much left of the first one's face that anyone would be able to recognize. Bart didn't enjoy the killing but it was becoming necessary now and he wasn't averse to doing what had to be done. The only hope the country had left was that citizens with honor and the courage to back it up would step up to put down the elements bent on its destruction. These looters might not be terrorists and insurrectionists like the worst of the lot that had started all this, but they were certainly contributing to the disorder and many of them were just as dangerous. Bart had been half expecting things to come to this for years, but when it finally happened the breakdown of law and order came much quicker and was far more widespread than even he could have imagined.

Wide scale riots and well-planned terror attacks that broke out almost simultaneously from coast to coast had the authorities reeling and citizens in panic mode. The worst part of it all was that no one knew who was going to strike next or where. Radical Islamic jihadists were responsible for some of it in the beginning, but emboldened by the results of their attacks, domestic anarchist groups determined to overthrow the government and get rid of anyone with whom they disagreed struck out at anything and anyone representing the authority they hated.

The government response, which was swift and forceful, only added fuel to the fire, leading to more violence and unrest, including outright defiance of federal authority by scores of cities and several entire states. With much of the nation's military power spread thin and depleted because of the wars in Europe and Asia, authority from Washington was being challenged on many fronts. Bart had always dismissed conspiracy theories, but the more he learned of this situation, the more convinced he became that the whole thing had been orchestrated to happen this way from the beginning. The divide that had been building for years between people with irreconcilable ideologies morphed into an unbridgeable chasm. War had come to America—not a conventional war against a common enemy—but a wild and unpredictable outbreak of guerrilla insurgency and insurrection between numerous factions, each with its own agenda. Wave after wave of mass shootings, bombings and vehicle attacks put nearly everyone on the front lines and overwhelmed law enforcement at every level. The truth of the matter was that there was so much going on across the country that few people knew the full extent of it. What news had been available had to be treated with suspicion because of all the propaganda being spread, and that was before south Florida was hit by the hurricane. Now, with most of the power and communications grid down from the storm, there had been little news of anything from the outside.

Before that latest disaster struck, Bart had been in semi-regular contact with Keith via ham radio. As rural as it was, even Keith's jurisdiction wasn't insulated from the violence. As a deputy sheriff of St. Martin Parish, he'd had his hands full with other problems before the storm and had little info to share. Most non-essential federal government agencies had shut down well before summer began and that included NOAA and the National Hurricane Center. There had been little warning the storm was coming other than sporadic reports spread through the amateur radio nets as it made its way through the islands of the West Indies. From what he could piece together of it, Bart figured the Miami-Fort Lauderdale area would get it the worst, and the last time he'd talked to Keith, Bart told him he was going by boat to North Palm Beach to get his granddaughter out of its path before the hurricane arrived.

He'd arrived to learn that Megan hadn't even made it home to Florida, but Bart convinced her mother and her stepdad and stepbrother to come back with him anyway. While hurricane-force winds hammered the entire peninsula all the way across to the Gulf, the direct impact danger was far less where Bart lived than on the Atlantic coast. They'd ridden it out okay, but the aftermath left a wake of destruction as severe as any hurricane Bart had experienced in three decades of south Florida living. The damage to the power grid and other infrastructure was irreparable in the present state of the nation, and Bart had no illusions that it would be fixed in the foreseeable future.

He had no way of knowing the path the storm took after it entered the Gulf, but he was certain it had re-strengthened over those warm waters as so many others before it had. If so, it had to make landfall again somewhere, most likely on the northern coast. Keith's AO in Louisiana could have taken as hard a hit as Florida—maybe even harder. Whatever the extent of the damage, Bart was certain that people surviving in the strike zones were on their own now, and would be for the foreseeable future. That wasn't as much of a problem for him as it was for most people, because Bart Branson was prepared. His three new houseguests were having a harder time dealing with it, but they were far better off here with him than anywhere else they could be in that part of the state. He was doing all he could for them, but like everyone else they were going to have to get used to a harsh new reality. The easy life most Americans had known had come to an end.

It was still nearly four hours until daylight when Bart put his camera away and carried the guns to his office to lock them up. He doubted anyone else would make an attempt on the yard before morning, but he was wired from the action and unable to relax anyway, so he took up his position again on the trawler and settled in to watch, just in case. When dawn came with no more excitement, Bart climbed down from his perch as he brushed away the morning swarms of biting no-see-ums from his face and neck. The rising sun would soon drive them away but they were always a nuisance at this hour on days when the wind was calm. He walked to the wet slips on the other side of the Travelift and stepped aboard the 18-foot aluminum skiff he kept tied up there. After warming up the outboard, he motored around to the little beach and eased his bow up onto the sand where the kayakers had landed their plastic boats. Bart wanted to get rid of the bodies first thing, in case someone came around the yard that morning, as unlikely as that might be. It was a chore, but he managed to drag them one at a time down to the water's edge next to his boat. Then he picked up a couple of old anchors and a half-rotten mooring line from his collection of cast-off gear piled near the slipway, and put the anchors in his boat. Bart tied each man's ankles together with short pieces he cut from the line and then he passed one end of the 20-foot remainder through the lashings, securing it with several half hitches before cleating the bitter end to the bow of the skiff. Once he was back aboard, he fired up the 50-horse Yamaha again and backed out into the river, dragging the dead men with him. A channel had been dredged here years ago to accommodate deep-draft vessels, so Bart didn't have to go far to find sufficient depths. He shackled the two anchors to the line between the cleat and the bodies and after taking the loops off the cleat, tied a couple of stopper knots to keep the shackles from slipping off the bitter end before dropping it into the murky brown water. Bart waited until the bodies sank out of sight before shifting the motor back into gear. The river provided a convenient and permanent means of disposal, especially with all the big gators that were about, and Bart suspected those two wouldn't be the last he would have to dump there.

He scanned the river upstream and down before heading back to the dock, not that he expected to see any traffic there this early in the morning. Few boats were moving at all these days, and those that were tended to do so during the midday hours, when most people perceived travel to be safer. Bart couldn't guard the boatyard day and night by himself, but it was generally safe to leave it and go home for a few hours during the day. He secured the skiff to the dock and went in his office to pour the last stale cup of coffee into his cup before washing out the pot and locking up to go home.

The last thing he did every morning before he left was climb aboard the Oyster 56 cutter in the yard to see if he could raise anybody or pick up some news transmissions on the ham radio. That boat had the best antenna set up of any in the yard, and Bart had managed to talk to some other operators in Florida but the repeaters in the area were still out of commission since the storm so he'd been unable to get through to anyone outside the immediate region. He was hopeful that someone would have something up and running soon so he could get back in touch with Keith, but it had been weeks now and today was no different. Bart downed the last of his coffee and shut off the station, then climbed down and headed for his skiff.

Bart's small house was just a mile and a half up the Caloosahatchee, a hip-roof bungalow set back from the river in a grove of coconut palms so dense it was completely hidden from the water. He had fallen in love with the place from the moment he laid eyes on it nearly thirty years ago, at the same time he realized that south Florida was where he wanted to be. Bart got his first taste of the tropics in Southeast Asia, and while many of his memories of that first tour in 1969 were quite unpleasant, there was something about the jungle and its exotic vegetation that spoke to his soul. Surrounded by his palms in a place winter barely touched, Bart found that feeling again on the Caloosahatchee. The house that came with his little three-acre wooded plot wouldn't be anything special to most folks, but it was just right for Bart. He loved the wrap-around porches that added 10 feet of outdoor living space on all four sides, with coconut fronds and giant philodendron leaves creating a screen of jungle greenery that would close in and consume the place if he left it unattended for long.

Bart spent most of his time at home living on those porches, equipped as they were with hammocks, rocking chairs, his barbecue grill, workbenches and a set of iron barbells in a squat rack to keep him strong. The house itself was just as rustic, with knotty-pine planked floors and cabinets and furniture Bart had handcrafted from reclaimed wood. He had a small bedroom in the upstairs loft and a kitchen and single bath shoehorned into the space below it, but the rest of the bungalow was just one big open room with a few shelves along the walls and lots of hooks and nails for hanging his miscellaneous possessions. It wasn't the kind of house most women would be interested in, but Bart didn't want a woman around full-time anyway. Making it work for his houseguests took a bit of rearranging, but Bart was happy sleeping in one of his hammocks or on a spare mattress he laid out on the floor in a corner, relinquishing his modest bedroom to his former daughter in law and her new husband.

Bart slowed the skiff to idle as he approached his property. Like the house, the small dock where he kept the skiff was invisible from the river. A narrow creek that bounded one side of the property entered the Caloosahatchee here, and created a perfect hideaway for his boat dock. Bart had used it almost daily the entire time he'd lived here, commuting by boat back and forth between the house and his boatyard. He had always valued the privacy this setup had offered over the years, but now it was a crucial element of his security. The river was an easy avenue for would-be looters and other dangerous folks, but if they didn't know the house was there, they had no reason to even slow down when they went by. With the situation being what it was now, Bart was extra careful to keep any noise low and to avoid lights at night that could be seen through the foliage. The front entrance that connected to a small county road was equally low-key, just a gravel road with an iron gate that from all appearances led to an undeveloped and unused parcel of land.

He checked the river both upstream and down, like he always did these days before turning off into the little side creek. It helped that his comings and goings were less frequent now, but so far he'd managed to get in and out without being seen by other river users. Bart tied off the skiff when he reached the dock and slung the M1 over his shoulder before stepping out. He was tired and ready to get some sleep, but with company in the house that wasn't easy in the daytime. Like every other day since they'd been here, he would talk with them a while and then try and get a long nap in his hammock that afternoon. Then come nightfall, he'd head back down to the yard and resume his solitary watch.

Eighteen

SHAUNA HARTFIELD HEARD THE sound of Bart's outboard turning into the creek and went outside to walk down to meet him at the dock. She was going stir crazy out here in the middle of nowhere, with no connection to the outside world, although she knew it wouldn't be any different at her house or anywhere else in south Florida. Each day when Bart returned from the boatyard, she hoped he would have some news—it didn't matter what—just news of any kind. The waiting and not knowing was the hardest part of this situation, mainly because of her worry over Megan, but also because of Daniel's apparent inability to cope that was wearing on her nerves more every day.

"No, I'm afraid not," Bart said, when Shauna asked if he'd spoken to anyone since he'd left the evening before. "I did have a couple of fellows drop by the yard a little after midnight, but they weren't the talkative type and never said a word."

Shauna knew without asking what Bart meant. He'd already told her about his previous encounters in the boatyard since they'd returned here from North Palm Beach. Her ex-father-in-law was deadly serious about keeping the looters off of his property, especially after what had happened to his two favorite employees. Shauna couldn't really blame him, but she didn't care to hear the details either, and Bart wouldn't volunteer them unless asked. But she did wonder how long he was going to keep doing this, as it was beginning to seem like there was little point in it.

"I wish you would give it a rest, Bart. You don't have to go out there every single night."

"Who else is going to if I don't? Somebody's got to stand up to these people. I can't just let 'em rob me blind."

"You can't be there all the time either, and you know it. If you're right about things getting even worse than they are now, then you're going to have to just let the boatyard go, just like we had to let our house go."

"I can hold them off for quite a while. The situation here is a whole lot different than over there on the other coast. You know that Shauna, even if Daniel doesn't understand it. Is he still talking about trying to go back to North Palm Beach this week?"

"It's all he *has* talked about. He says he doesn't want to go without me, but that he will if he has to. He's got Andrew convinced it's a good idea too."

"You know what I think of it, and he does too. If he wants to try it, I'm not going to stop him, but I'll be damned if I'm going to do a whole lot to help him either. He's a fool to put that boy at risk like that when we've all got everything we need right here."

"Well, he still can't grasp the fact that the grid could stay down this long in a place like Palm Beach County. He thinks things are different there because it's not out in the sticks like here. I guess he'll have to see for himself to believe it, but I don't think he'd ever make it over there. All I can do is keep trying to talk him out of it, and I know you're sick of it, but I need your help, Bart. I'm trying to keep him calm, but it makes me mad because he has no idea what *I'm* going through. He's worried about a stupid house and all the money and investments he can't get to and maybe never will again, but he has no idea what it's like to have a child that's hopelessly out of reach and maybe in grave danger. I know *you* understand, Bart, but I don't think Daniel really gets it."

Shauna knew Bart was genuinely concerned about his granddaughter's whereabouts and safety, which was why he made the perilous drive across the state to get them before the storm. But looking for her now wasn't really an option. Assuming she was still in the Boulder area where she was attending the university, getting to her to bring her back was no simple matter. Travel had been dangerous and severely restricted for months even before the hurricane, and cell phones and other forms of communications had become sporadic and unreliable at best. When Shauna lost touch with

Megan and she didn't come home at the end of the semester, Daniel had urged her to sit tight and wait. He was sure that things would settle down and Megan would be fine if she stayed put where she was. Megan was practically an adult; after all, while her stepson Andrew was only twelve. She was the only mother he had now, his real mother taken by cancer when he was eight. Shauna couldn't bail on her responsibility to be there for him and Daniel, nor could she expect the two of them to accompany her on a risky journey across half a continent. Besides, with no way to communicate her intentions to Megan, there was a good chance they would miss each other in transit if Megan attempted to come home on her own.

Whether or not she would even try was a whole different topic. Shauna had left a note for her in her bedroom at home just in case, but she had her doubts. She didn't discuss all the reasons with Bart because he had not been around his granddaughter much since she'd graduated high school. Knowing her better than anyone else, Shauna had good reason to worry when the first incidents of the insurrection began making the news shortly after the beginning of the year. She sincerely hoped that her daughter would steer clear of the protests and riots, but knowing her as she did, she doubted it. As the weeks went by with no word from her, Shauna's worry only increased, but hopping on a flight to go out and visit as she'd done twice during Megan's freshman year was no longer an option. The government had put an indefinite halt to commercial airline operations and even overland travel was highly restricted. Driving within the state had been possible before the hurricane, but interstate travel was much more problematic, especially with the gas shortages that worsened by the week.

Since she could do nothing for Megan at the moment, Shauna kept telling herself that her daughter was no doubt surrounded by friends that would look out for one another. That had worked to get her through most of the summer, but it was getting harder to take the not knowing. Now that she and Daniel and Andrew had been displaced from their home by the storm, she had even more time to think and worry. She believed Bart when he said there was nothing to go back to in North Palm Beach. Even if the house was undamaged by the storm, it would be uninhabitable in the Florida heat without electricity and air conditioning. At least Bart's house was designed for the climate and built to be sustainable off grid. The palms that hid it from view of the river also shaded it on all sides, contributing greatly to keeping it cool. Water wasn't an issue because Bart had a well with a pump that could be run on his generators or manually. Then, of course, there was always the creek from which more could be collected as a last resort. All in all, there was no comparison between the livability of Bart's remote bungalow and Shauna and Daniel's waterfront suburban home in North Palm

Beach. Going back there in the foreseeable future simply wasn't an option, and Shauna knew they were leaving for good even as they packed up to go with Bart.

She knew too as she was writing her note to Megan that her daughter would probably never read it, but it made her feel better to do *something.* Even now she wrote letters to Megan every day. It didn't matter that she had no means to send them; just the act of writing to her made Shauna feel closer. It gave her someone to confide in too, mostly of her disappointment in Daniel.

Her second husband was completely out of his element in this situation and his complaints and useless worries were making things harder than they had to be. The man excelled in the world of business and corporate management, but was utterly incompetent when it came to dealing with the conditions they now faced. Shauna could have guessed that before she married him, but she'd seriously doubted it would ever matter. What *did* matter then was that he was nice to her and Megan and he was always there for them, unlike Eric, who had rarely been. Daniel was confident and successful in the world he knew before the collapse, but with far less of the cockiness and aggression that Eric had cultivated in his own intense occupation.

Shauna had been glad for the change when she met her new husband, but considering what she was facing now, she couldn't help but compare the two men. Like his father Bart,

Eric would do what had to be done and would be quick to adapt to hard circumstance as required. He would also find a way to get to his daughter, no matter what obstacles stood in his way, if only he were here to know she was missing. That was what Shauna wanted to believe anyway, but she had to acknowledge that the selfish bastard *wasn't* here, nor had he been for most of Megan's life. Instead of finding a way to be with his family and be a father to his only daughter, he'd made a career of killing fanatics in the most godforsaken countries on the planet. A part of her understood why, but the part that wanted him home as a husband and father thought he'd done more than his part in those endless wars, and that enough was enough.

And now, even though the terrorism and war had come home to America, Eric had not. Shauna thought that if she ever saw him again, the first thing she would do would be to walk up to him and slap him across the face. And if Daniel didn't get his act together soon, she would let him have the same. As it was, Bart Branson was the only man in her life she could depend on, and she was trying her best to be patient as he suggested, waiting until they had more information to make a plan for their next move.

"We're gonna figure out something, Shauna, we've just got to get more intel on the situation outside of Florida. It won't do Megan any good if we wind up getting arrested and put away in some detention camp trying to get there. I keep hoping every day that I'll be able to get through to Keith or someone else that can fill us in. That's as good a reason as I need to go out there every night and keep watch over that boatyard."

"I know you're right. It's just that it's killing me to wait here doing *nothing*." Shauna said. "Megan could be in far more danger than we are and we wouldn't even know it."

"You're not just doing nothing, Shauna. You're surviving, and that's a top priority. You can't help Megan or anyone else if you don't do that. That's all any of us can do at the moment. You've got to understand that and make peace with it. If you take care of yourself then you *will* be able to help Megan. But going off blind without a plan would just be foolish."

Shauna knew Bart's logic made sense, but that still didn't make her feel much better about what she was and wasn't doing. Megan was her child, even if she *was* almost twenty years old, and it was her job to worry about her. She walked with Bart back up to the house along the palm-shaded gravel pathway leading from the dock. Bart was carrying his rifle on a sling over one shoulder, and when they went inside, he hung it on its rack above the main doorway.

Shauna always felt better in the isolated house when Bart was at home. The long nights while he was away guarding his boatyard were somewhat spooky, as she knew it would be up to her to defend herself as well as Daniel and Andrew if anyone happened upon the house in the dark. Shauna still had the Glock 19 that Eric had given her years before, and under his expert instruction she had become quite proficient with it. It was the same model Eric carried everyday as his combat sidearm, and he had taught Megan how to shoot it as well, promising to buy her one of her own as soon as she turned eighteen and moved off to college. But that never happened because Shauna and Eric were divorced by the time Megan turned thirteen, and she had a new stepdad by the time she was fifteen. Daniel Hartfield wasn't a gun person and didn't own firearms of any kind. He'd barely tolerated Shauna's Glock when they got together, not seeing the point of it and considering its presence in the house a grave danger to his young son. Shauna refused to give it up, but did her best to keep it out of sight and out of mind. She knew part of her new husband's objection to the Glock was simple insecurity, no matter what he told her. Daniel knew the handgun came from Eric, and that he had taught Shauna to use it, and use it well—something he could never do. Eric Branson wasn't just another one of those stereotypical gun enthusiasts who liked to show off his toys to his buddies. The man had acquired and tested his skills on the battlefield, fighting with one of the most elite Special Ops units on the planet.

Daniel wouldn't admit that it still bothered him, but there were times when Shauna knew it did, especially in these last few days. The Glock was always on her belt when Bart was away from the house, and Daniel couldn't help but be aware that his petite wife was the only thing standing between him and Andrew and the violence unfolding around them. He had finally come to the point where he realized that it was time he and Andrew learned how to use firearms, but Bart wasn't ready to let them start target practice just yet. Even the .22 rifles he had available might draw unwanted attention from the river, so their introduction to weapons consisted of field stripping and handling, and practicing loading, unloading and dry firing until they could do better.

As for Megan, the breakup of her parents' marriage ended any chance of her continuing interest in shooting. None of her friends in high school were into it and by then Megan encountered teachers that brought into question everything she'd ever known about her dad. She became convinced that what he was doing with his life was misguided and wrong and that he'd been fighting unjust wars in the service of a government driven only by corruption and greed. Megan no longer believed her dad was protecting his country from terrorism, and she certainly no longer believed that she was in any danger from that threat at home. She had carried those beliefs with her when she left to attend the university, and Shauna had little doubt that Megan would become even more entrenched in that way of thinking while living on campus. She knew Megan had a lot to figure out for herself though, and trying too hard to influence her thinking would only make matters worse. It was her dream to go to the university in Boulder, partly because of the dramatic difference in landscape and climate and partly because her best friend, Allison, was going there too. Shauna was also quite certain that some of the attraction of Colorado was the legal high that had nothing to do with the mountains, but she couldn't stop Megan from doing that whether she was here or out there. Her stepfather's generosity removed any obstacles to funding the education of her choice, so the decision had been made before she graduated high school. If what had happened over the last six months had caused any changes in Megan's thinking, it was too late to make a difference now. As far as Shauna knew, her daughter still had no means to protect herself, in a country where unprecedented violence raged from coast to coast.

Nineteen

BART WAS IN NO mood to deal with Daniel Hartfield after being up all night guarding the yard. Shauna had already told him what to expect though, and he was ready when Daniel started in on him again about traveling to North Palm Beach.

"I've been thinking of alternatives, Bart. I know it's too risky to travel the roads, even in your truck, and I know you said the Okeechobee Waterway through the lake probably isn't open to traffic. But what if we used one of the large motor cruisers from down there in your boatyard? We could go down the river to the Gulf and then around the tip of Florida and back up to North Palm Beach. I could pay for everything. I can certainly compensate the owner of whatever boat we use, or even buy it outright once things are straightened out with the banks. What do you think about that? I think it would be far less risky because there won't be many people out there once we get to open water."

"There ain't no way in hell, is what I think about it! There's no telling what kind of bandits we'd run into just between here and Fort Myers, much less along the coast. It won't matter if we're in a big boat or a small one, we'd just be a target of opportunity for anyone that sees us."

"Well we've got to do *something!* We can't just sit here day after day, week after week, doing *nothing!*"

"We *are* doing something! We're staying alive, that's what we're doing! That's better than a lot of folks can expect, I'll tell you that! This is as good a place as you are going to find anywhere in south Florida, I can assure you, but there are no guarantees even here. Now why would you want to go and risk the lives of your wife and son trying to get over there to the east coast that's been torn up by a damned hurricane? You may not take the dangers that are out there seriously, but you need to start thinking about them!"

"You don't know that the hurricane did that much damage. All we know is what we've seen here. You're just guessing when you say there's nothing left to go back to over there. I can assure you, no hurricane damage is going to prevent what are some of the wealthiest communities in the United States from making a quick recovery. Things may be better over there already than they are here. They probably even have the power back on by now."

Bart just stared at this man his former daughter-in-law had married with a blank expression on his face. How anyone could be so delusional in the face of harsh reality was beyond him, and he didn't have the patience to argue with him.

"Okay Daniel. If you want to buy one of the boats out of my yard, bring me the cash and I'll set her over in the river for you. Then you can have at it, but I'm not going. If you want to take your son, that's fine. If Shauna wants to go with you, that's fine too, but I'm having no part of it!"

"Cash? How do you think I can get ahold of that much cash right now? Yes, I can get it later, after we get back home, but you know as well as I do that the situation with the banks is going to take some time to sort out. Shauna knows what I'm worth though. She will assure you I'm good for it, whatever amount we settle on."

"We ain't settling on nothing without cash money. I'm responsible for every vessel that's in that yard. One day the owners are going to show up wanting them back, and I'll be damned if I'm going to tell one of them I let some fellow that was 'good for it' take his boat on credit!"

In truth, Bart doubted that most of the owners would ever show up there again. If it were indeed feasible to pay them, he figured most of them would gladly sell out of their yachts that were unlikely to ever do them any good again. Bart knew there were quite a few large boat owners that were already well prepared and ready to go that probably got out of the country while the getting was good. A well-equipped cruiser, especially if it was set up and provisioned for long voyages, would make a damned fine alternative to holing up in any of the cities, hoping for the best. A few of the vessels in his yard met the requirements for that kind of escape, but most were in various stages of refit or in need of it, and in other cases the owners lived far away, storing their boats here for their annual winter jaunts in warm waters. Those folks several states away would surely never make it back, at least until things changed drastically. But regardless of all that, Daniel Hartfield didn't have the knowledge or the experience to do what he was proposing without Bart's help, and Bart had zero interest in trying to go back to the east coast of Florida.

The bottom line was that Bart was in no mood to waste anymore time discussing it. If Shauna's husband didn't get it yet, Bart figured he probably never would. He figured there were plenty of folks just like him all over the country—the kind of folks that couldn't understand what they were really facing. Life as they knew it before wasn't coming back anytime soon, and not just because of a hurricane, either. Things had gone too far this time for an easy fix, but of course people didn't want to hear it. Most of them had never known hard times, much less the kind of hard times Bart knew was coming. Shauna was handling it well though, especially considering how worried she was about her daughter. Bart had always liked her and had done his best to talk some sense into Eric before the woman finally gave up on him. He understood his son's sense of duty and the lure of being part of a really special team of top-notch operators, but

Bart agreed with Shauna that Eric had done his part. He should have come home to stay ten years ago. Shauna wanted someone that would be there for her and her daughter, and Bart couldn't blame her. He didn't have anything against Daniel Hartfield for stepping in and taking his son's place; someone was bound to anyway. Shauna was a beautiful woman with a great personality, and Bart hadn't expected her to remain single for long. Her new husband provided nicely for her and all had been well before all this chaos and disorder began. Daniel simply wasn't equipped to deal with that, and Bart knew most people weren't. They didn't prepare for such things because they didn't believe such things could ever happen.

Bart went back outside to sit down for a minute with Shauna and Andrew before he turned in for a few hours of sleep. He knew the boy was having a hard time too, and it didn't help to hear his father and stepmother arguing over what they ought to do. Shauna had made him breakfast and was trying to keep him distracted from the conversation Bart had just had with his father. Bart knew the kid was bound to have his doubts as to who was right about all this, but overall he was taking it as good as could be expected. The biggest problem Andrew was dealing with was the sheer boredom. It was a long time since Bart had been 12 years old, but he could well remember how easily a boy could get bored with just sitting around waiting, and how time seemed to drag so much slower at that age. It was even worse for kids now, because they were used to passing the time with video games and other electronic forms of entertainment. Andrew still had his smartphone with some game apps installed, and keeping it charged wasn't a problem when they were running the generator. But there was no way to connect to the Internet to download anything new, so he was still bored, even with that.

"Are you going to let us start target shooting today?" Andrew asked, hopefully.

"I wish I could, son, but I'm afraid it's still not a very good idea right now. There are still a lot of strangers making their way up and down the river, and we just don't have anything to offer them if they come asking for help."

Bart didn't really think the sound of gunfire would attract the kind of people that would actually ask for help, but it would sure attract attention, which was the last thing they needed. It was a good thing that Andrew and his father wanted to learn to shoot though, because Bart knew something could happen to him, leaving their security totally up to Shauna if they didn't. He'd promised Andrew he would figure out a way to get them started as soon as he could. He knew a couple of isolated spots they could go in the skiff to where they could get in some target practice, but it would be best to do that at night, and on an evening when there was enough moonlight to see what they were doing. Right now, with what had just happened last night in the boatyard, Bart wasn't willing to leave the property unattended after dark.

"I hate sitting around here all day with nothing to do. I wish I could go with you and help you guard the boatyard tonight. I can be quiet, I promise."

"Not tonight, Andrew, but one of these nights soon, I'll take you down there. I know it's boring having to wait sometimes, but we'll go do some more fishing late this afternoon after I catch up on my sleep."

"Fishing's boring too, just sitting on the riverbank hoping something will bite. I like fishing in the boat out in the ocean a lot better. Even behind our house is better, because you never know what you're going to catch in the canal. I don't like this freshwater fishing in that stupid little creek. It's always the same old thing. Do you really think we won't ever be able to go back to our house? I heard what you told my dad, but he says we can. He says we ought to at least go and see. I wish we could."

"Believe me, Andrew, I wish we could too. If this was just a hurricane we were dealing with, we would be able to soon. There'd be power companies sending trucks and crews in from all over the Southeast. I've seen it time after time when a hurricane hits. There'd be search and rescue teams and volunteer groups bringing in food, water, generators and everything you can imagine that would be needed, and things would have already been looking a lot better by now. But this isn't just a hurricane, and you know that as well as I do. Those folks from out of state aren't coming, because they can't. Maybe eventually, when law and order is restored, they'll get around to getting the power back on down here, but it could be months before that happens, and the more folks suffer in the meantime, the more dangerous some of them will become."

Bart stopped when he caught Shauna's glare. She had already gotten onto him about scaring the boy, but Bart didn't see that twelve years old was too young to deal with reality. The truth was, if Andrew was going to survive now, he was going to have to grow up fast. Bart knew it was possible, because he'd seen it firsthand. Hell, he'd encountered kids younger than that fighting with the Viet Cong. Whether Shauna and Daniel agreed with it or not, Bart wasn't about to sugarcoat the truth and keep the boy in the dark. Spending time alone with him fishing was a good opportunity to talk to him and to begin his real education, and yes, when the time was right, he would take him to the boatyard. The kid was going to be exposed to the violence one way or the other, Bart was certain of that, and he would do his part to get him prepared for it. Regardless of how traumatic that might prove to be, it was far preferable to what Bart was certain many kids Andrew's age must have already had to face during these trying times.

He excused himself from their company and went around to the porch on the west side of the house to his hammock. That was his best bet for undisturbed daytime sleep, as there was too much commotion in the house with his guests moving about, no matter how quiet they tried to be. Bart didn't need much sleep these days anyway. It seemed the older he got, the harder it was to sleep more than a few hours, so it hadn't been difficult to adapt to his new schedule of watching the yard all night and napping by day. The west side of the porch was coolest in the mornings, and by the time it started warming in the middle of the afternoon, Bart was usually ready to eat something and do his afternoon chores. After that, fishing the creek with Andrew for an hour or two before sunset was something to look forward to before he left again for the boatyard.

Twenty

BART TOOK HIS SPRINGFIELD down off the rack and left the house again at about ten minutes after sundown. He stood waiting and listening on his dock for several minutes, hidden from view of anyone on the river by the dense trees that hung out over the banks of the little side creek. After deciding all was clear on the river, he started the outboard and cast off, doing a quick visual upstream and down to confirm the river was deserted as he entered the main channel. When he arrived at the yard, he made a round along the perimeter and did a walkthrough of the rows of blocked-up vessels, checking that all was as he left it that morning. So far, there had been no pillaging during daylight hours, but Bart knew it could happen anytime, and was bound to eventually. He couldn't be there twenty-four seven though, even if he could stay awake, not with Shauna and her family at his house, demanding part of his attention.

He opened up his little office and put a pot of water to boil on the propane stove for coffee. When his brew was ready, he filled his insulated travel mug and made his way over to the trawler that had become his guard post and lookout tower. As he settled in for another long night, Bart reflected back over the conversations of the day, first with Shauna, and then with Daniel and Andrew. Despite her worries over Megan, Shauna was handling all this better than most in her shoes could. The more that Bart was around her, the more he knew his son was a fool for letting her get away. Not only was she smart and levelheaded under duress, Bart also thought she was even better looking now at thirty-nine than she'd been when she was his daughter-in-law. Eric had to know what he was giving up, and Bart couldn't figure out why he would do it. As far as he knew, Shauna had been as patient with him as a woman could be, especially considering all the worry that the man had put her through being gone more often than not. Bart couldn't blame her for wanting more, and he was sure that Daniel Hartfield had been good to her, but he could also see the disappointment in him written all over her face now, as it was obvious that the man was unwilling to accept that the world he'd known was no longer there to go back to. Bart understood that they were all growing anxious and impatient, although each of them for different reasons. Sitting in that secluded bungalow day after day, night after night was getting old, especially for folks used to a fast-paced life in the city. Without electricity, land-lines or cell phone communications, they were cut off from the outside world, stuck in the middle of nowhere with little to distract them from their worries and boredom.

All these factors were causing inevitable tension, and Bart didn't really know what to do about it. He was doing the best he could by providing them a refuge that was relatively safe. They might be doing without a lot of what they were used to, but they were sheltered from the weather and had plenty to eat. The latter was especially a big deal now, considering how many people in this part of the state must be going hungry by now. Grocery store shelves had already been mostly depleted because of the riots and disruption of transportation long before the hurricane. Bart had been moving supplies from some of the yachts to his house for weeks, and there was even more where that came from, still tucked away in the lockers of most of them. Because so many of them were long-distance cruising vessels designed to be self-sufficient, they were well stocked with non-perishable goods. Having access to them in his boatyard was like having his own mini disaster preparation center. The folks that had stored all that stuff aboard their vessels wouldn't likely be back to claim it, so Bart intended to make use of as much as he and his guests needed. In his mind it wasn't stealing, because he'd contracted to provide storage for the vessels as well as performing maintenance and repairs on most of them. And despite the circumstances, he was still managing to provide security, even though it meant watching over the yard at night with his rifle. If things ever returned to normal, which Bart doubted, he'd settle up with the boat owners by deducting what he'd taken from their bills. Since those invoices would likely never be delivered, the food and other goods he salvaged was likely the only compensation he'd ever get for his diligent efforts, and Bart was glad he had company to help him make use of it. Bart knew that if he didn't have these resources, things would indeed be tough, but he figured he could probably get by for a while off of fishing the river and whatnot. As it was, what little fishing he was doing was just a pastime and diversion for Andrew.

Bart had kept his promise to the boy earlier that day, when he woke from his nap. Every afternoon, it was much the same. They would go down and sit on the bank of the little creek next to his dock, casting for bass with artificial lures and using cane poles with cork bobbers on the line in hopes of catching a catfish or bream. It wasn't a very exciting way to fish for a 12-year-old boy, especially one who'd been offshore fishing in the Atlantic. At least it gave Andrew something to look forward to every though; something besides hanging around the house all day, listening to the same old conversations between his dad and stepmom. Bart did his best to make it interesting for him, telling him tales of things that had happened on the river and stories of the days when the Everglades took in all of the state south of Lake

Okeechobee. It was a distraction for him until they could do something more exciting, like shooting the guns for real.

These thoughts occupied his mind as the hours slipped by, and Bart was beginning to think it was going to be a quiet, uneventful night—something he wouldn't complain about one bit. He got up walked around the deck of the trawler a couple hours before dawn, stretching his legs and thinking about going down to the office to heat up the rest of the coffee. But when he glanced back out at the river, he caught a glimpse of movement several hundred yards downstream. Sweeping the dark water with his riflescope, Bart studied the area in question, thinking maybe it was just a low-flying heron or some other large shorebird early off the roost. But then he saw it again, magnified in the scope, and recognized the rhythmic up and down motion for what it was—*kayak paddles!* The water reflected off the surface of the blades in such a way that they were visible even in the darkness, giving away the location of the silent craft sneaking upriver. Bart scanned the channel on both sides of the flashing paddles but didn't see anything to indicate there was another one. What he could tell now though, was that there were two paddlers sitting in tandem in the one, so it was a bigger kayak than the little solo sit-on-tops the two fellows arrived in the night before. It was hard to see the details, because the boat itself was either black or very dark in color, and the men paddling it were also wearing dark clothing. There was little doubt in

Bart's mind that these two fellows were up to no good though, and when the boat began gradually angling across the river straight in the direction of the boatyard, his suspicions were confirmed. *Well just come on, you damned sons of bitches! Come on and get you some of what your buddies got last night! I imagine those gators won't mind another good feeding, and besides, I've got enough ammo to do this every night—probably for the rest of my life!*

Although he could have easily taken them out while they were still in the boat, Bart was going to give these two the benefit of the doubt just like all the rest. He would wait and see what they did once they landed on the boatyard property, even though he was already quite certain they were here to loot and steal. *Why else would anyone sneak upriver to come here at this hour?*

Bart moved the crosshairs of the scope back and forth between the two figures as they pulled up to the narrow beach, but their faces were in the shadows, and he could tell little about them. The one in the bow seat got out with a line in hand to tie off the kayak to a nearby piling, while the other man stepped out into the water at the stern to help him pull it ashore. When it was far enough up on the beach to not float away, that same man in the rear reached into the kayak and got out a black rifle, which he handed to his partner before retrieving another one of his own. The weapons appeared to be compact AR-15 type rifles from the silhouettes he could see, and if he wasn't mistaken, it looked like one of them even had a grenade launcher attached. *What in the hell?*

But Bart was more curious about their boat than their choice of weapons. He could tell that it was one of the folding type kayaks that he had seen in Florida waters before on occasion, but the matte black finish wasn't typical. Bart wondered if it came that way or if these two thieves had painted it black to aid in their stealthy nighttime raids. If the latter were the case, then they were serious about their occupation and this certainly wasn't their first target. Once again, he considered taking them out now before they took another step into his yard, but he would wait until there was no question he was justified. But whenever he did it, he would get both of them quickly, before either had a chance to return fire.

Bart expected to see them pull out the tools they would need for breaking and entering next, but they did not. Once they secured their boat they just stood there next to the kayak, apparently discussing something and in no particular hurry to begin what they came for. Bart wondered which of the dry-docked yachts they were going to select first, but when they finally started walking, they made a beeline straight for his office instead. What they expected to find in there he had no idea, but he figured he would get a chance for a clean shot once they reached the door. Anticipating this in advance, Bart quickly crawled across the bow of the trawler to set up in a better position to take them out. He decided that their first attempt to breech the door would be his signal to open fire, and from the looks of it, he wouldn't have long to wait.

When the two men reached the small concrete porch in front of the entrance, they each leaned up to the small window near the top of the metal door and looked in. There was nothing to see in the dark room inside, but Bart figured they were probably making sure no one was around before they began to break in. It was odd that they didn't have a crowbar or something with them to do it, but then again, maybe they were planning to find something handy in the yard.

The first one that had gotten out of the kayak was standing nearest to him, and when he turned to look around at the surrounding boats, Bart brought the reticle of his scope onto his face. The light was much better here, and with the 4x magnification, he could see that the fellow was young, maybe even a teenager. Longish brown hair framed his gaunt-looking face, and even though he was unshaven, his beard and mustache was sparse, barely forming a shadow over his boney features. He was thin all over, but whether that was from going hungry since the hurricane or just his natural, underdeveloped state, Bart couldn't tell.

So far, he hadn't gotten a good look at his partner's face. He did notice that the other one had a heavier beard though, and figured he might be older. Maybe the two of them were brothers, or perhaps even father and son. Bart didn't know why he thought of it, because it certainly didn't matter. He didn't care who they were. The minute they attempted to break in that office or touch one of his boats, they were going to pay the ultimate price for their bad decisions.

When the older-looking man stepped off the porch and disappeared around the corner of the building, Bart figured he was looking for something with which to punch out the glass so he could reach in and unlock the door. There was no shortage of scrap metal and chunks of two-by-fours and other lumber scattered around with which he could accomplish that task, and it would no doubt be just a minute or two more before it was time to shoot. While he waited, Bart watched the young fellow as he stood there looking around, holding the black rifle in his hands as if he expected to need it. Bart already knew the rifles they carried were variants of that popular design he so despised, but he would add them to his growing collection anyway. The other fellow that was out of sight had the one with the grenade launcher. If it was real and he had any live rounds for it, it could make a good addition to his arsenal. But if nothing else, the rifles would probably come in handy as trade goods somewhere farther down the line.

Bart waited, wondering what was taking the man so long when there were so many things available that he could pick up to smash out a window. He was ready to get this over with. It was less than two hours until dawn and by the time he did the shooting and dragged the bodies to the water and disposed of them, he would come close to running out of darkness. Another couple minutes passed before the man finally returned, and when he did, Bart saw that he was still empty handed. His rifle in its sling was pushed off to one side, and he was adjusting his belt, as if he'd simply stepped around there to take a leak. The young fellow was saying something to him when the man finished with his belt and reached for the doorknob as if to test the lock. Bart brought the reticle onto the side of his head, centering his aim point just in front of the man's left ear. His finger was taking up the slack in the trigger as he slowed his breathing and put all of his focus into the target. He was only waiting until the man forced the door, and as soon as he did, he would die. Bart certainly didn't want a situation where one or both of them were holed up inside his office with rifles and maybe even a grenade launcher, because that would be a far more difficult problem to solve. Better to kill them both now, while they were still outside in the open. Bart felt the firmness of the trigger against the pad of his index finger, and then the man turned to speak to his partner, moving his face slightly out the crosshairs. His first instinct was to simply realign them between his target's eyes, and Bart did. He wouldn't have thought about the face itself, but for some reason he allowed himself to study it for a second. What he saw when he did caused him to break out in a cold sweat; his hands trembling as he carefully eased his finger away from the trigger. *He had almost shot his firstborn son! The man in his crosshairs was Eric Branson!*

Twenty-one

BART PLACED HIS RIFLE on the deck beside him and pulled himself up to his knees, still shaking from adrenalin as he realized what he'd nearly done. Eric and the young fellow with him were totally oblivious to his presence until he called out to them.

"ERIC! What the hell are you doing sneaking into my yard in the dark like this? You nearly got yourself shot, boy!"

"DAD! Is that you? Where are you?"

Bart saw them scanning their surroundings, looking for him among the nearby boats.

"Up here, Eric! You ought to know I'd pick an elevated position, given a choice. Wait where you are, I'm coming down!"

Eric and the young fellow with him didn't wait though. They were at the bottom of the ladder before Bart even reached the ground. He stepped off the last rung and turned around to find himself trapped in a giant bear hug, his son lifting him completely off the ground as Bart wrapped his own arms around him in turn.

"What in the hell are you doing sitting up there with a rifle at this hour you crazy old man?" Eric asked when he let him go and stepped back to look him over.

"Been having a problem with looters, what else? It's been going on ever since the hurricane, and I sure thought you two were more of the same. Now you tell me; where in the hell did you come from and how'd you get here? And who's your buddy you've got with you?"

"This kid? Oh, this is just Jonathan." Eric slapped Jonathan on the back. "I don't even know his last name. Have you got a last name, Jonathan?"

"Of course I do. It's Coleman, not that it matters. You never told me yours either." Jonathan turned back to Bart and extended his hand. "It's good to meet you, sir. I've heard a lot about you from Eric."

Bart shook it as he looked him over, not quite sure what to make of the boy. It was obvious he wasn't someone that had been working with Eric overseas, but at least he was respectful.

"He's just a beach bum I picked up on the coast near Jupiter Inlet," Eric grinned. "When I first met the punk, he tried to steal my kayak, but he's all right. He's a pretty good paddler and a helluva fisherman. He helped me sail a little Catalina 25 all the way around from Jupiter to the Keys and up to Fort Myers."

"What are you doing in that kayak then? Didn't have an engine on the Catalina?"

"We did, and enough gas to get up here too, but I didn't figure they would let us through the blockade, so we didn't ask. I didn't have any more use for the boat anyway, and it was pretty rough, so we set it adrift."

"Blockade? What blockade are you talking about?"

"The one at Fort Myers. Right there at the mouth of the Caloosahatchee. You didn't know about it?"

"No. That's the first I've heard of it. They must have done that after the hurricane, because until it hit, there were still folks coming upriver from the Gulf looking for a place to haul-out before it got here."

"What about Megan, Dad? Is she here with you?"

Bart saw the desperate hope in his son's eyes. This was the real reason he was here, and Bart hated to have to break the bad news to him. "No, I'm sorry son, she's not. When I knew for sure that the hurricane was going to hit us here in south Florida, I got in the truck and drove over there to Shauna's house to see if I could get them out. I was lucky to make it through, to tell you the truth, but when I got there, Shauna said she hadn't heard from Megan all summer and that as far as she knew, she was still in Colorado. I went ahead and brought Shauna and Daniel and his boy with me, because I knew it wasn't safe for them to stay there that close to the Atlantic. They're up at the house right now and have been ever since. That Daniel is about to drive me crazy with his wanting to go back to check on his house, but I've been telling him things over there are a hell of a lot worse than they are here. They may not have gotten a direct hit where they lived, but it had to be close, considering the path that hurricane took through here."

Eric took the news about Megan as if he'd already expected it. Bart knew he'd been hoping, but his son had seen plenty of disappointment in his life, and surely was prepared for more of the same. "You're right about the damage, Dad. I've been there. I went straight to Shauna's house as soon as I got to the coast. The house wasn't destroyed, but it's uninhabitable and it's been broken into and looted. Hell, the entire neighborhood has been looted and now it's deserted. There's no power anywhere over there and it is extremely dangerous to be out and about, even traveling by water at night."

Bart wasn't really surprised when Eric briefly related what he'd witnessed from right under Shauna's dock that night before he left the neighborhood. It had to be bad in places with that many desperate survivors, because it had been bad enough here. He told Eric of the incident right here in the yard, when thieves who took a motor yacht from one of the wet slips murdered his two long-time employees while he was away. Others had come after them, but Bart had been ready and waiting, just like tonight.

"So what's the story of that sneaky-looking black kayak that almost got you shot? Where'd you get it, son? And how did you get back from over there, wherever in the hell you've been working lately?"

"Heck, I paddled back, old man. What'd you think I did?"

Bart just laughed. "Knowing you, I about half believe it."

"I probably could have, if I'd had enough time. That thing can handle rough water like you wouldn't believe! But seriously, from the few reports I managed to get about what was happening here, I knew it was time to get my ass back ASAP. From what I could gather of the situation here, I figured I was going to need stuff that wouldn't be easy to bring in, if you know what I mean." Eric patted the rifle slung at his side and nodded at the one Jonathan carried. "A while back, I did a job where we used the kayaks to sneak into the coast, and it worked out well. I liked it so much I kept that one as part of my bonus for the operation and had it packed away in storage ever since. When I decided it was time to come home, I worked out a deal with a petroleum company to do a security hitch on one of their tankers in exchange for my passage. They agreed to drop me off near the east coast close to Jupiter, so the kayak was perfect. I'd heard all the ports were locked down anyway, even if I hadn't needed to slip my stuff in, and you probably know flying wasn't an option."

"Well I'll be damned. Leave it to you to figure out something as clever as that. Just so you know though, as sneaky as that thing may be, I had you in my sights long before you even landed. I could have taken you out before you touched the bank if I'd wanted to."

"I'm sure you could have, but not everybody's hardcore enough to sit up all night watching the river with an M1-A. I guess it's a good thing you had the courtesy to wait and catch us in the act before pulling the trigger."

"It's been my policy ever since this crap started. No reason to change that now. By the way, I've got a couple of kayaks now myself as of last night. Got 'em off a couple of fellows that stopped by around midnight, that's why when I saw you coming, I thought it was a new trend. They're nothing fancy, like yours, but the price was right."

"How many rounds?"

"I don't know, half a dozen? Who's counting anyway? I've got plenty more where those came from."

Eric grinned, but then his face turned serious as Bart opened up his office and flipped on the 12-volt-powered lighting. He could see that Eric's thoughts had returned to his daughter again, as she was the reason he was here.

"You said Shauna hasn't heard from Megan all summer? Have the phones really been down that long?"

"The cellular networks have. I don't know about all landlines, but how would you ever reach a kid on a landline these days anyway? Most Internet access was shut down too, but there were still ways to communicate, at least before the hurricane hit. They couldn't shut down ham radio, and that's what most of us were using, but that didn't do Megan any good, if she even thought about it. I doubt she knew anyone out there with a station."

"From what Jonathan's told me and the rumors I'd heard before I got here, driving out there's not really an option, is it Dad?"

"No, not at all. You'd never make it through, not traveling that far…when it first started, maybe… but not now. Even if you tried to stay on back roads all the way and avoided most of the checkpoints, you couldn't count on getting gas. And if you tried to carry enough with you for a trip like that, you'd be a prime target everywhere you went. Shauna and I have talked about it every day. Of course she would like to go and get Megan, but she understands how unrealistic that is right now. She'd been hoping Megan would show up all summer, but since the hurricane hit, she's hoping she stays put.

"What in the hell has become of this country, Dad? How did it come to this just since I was here last? What was it, a year and half ago?"

"About that, I reckon. You know as well as I do that it's been building up a lot longer than that, though. It's been like a pot about to boil over, the lid rattling under the pressure of the steam, until finally, it just blows off."

"There was more to it than a bunch of protesters starting riots on college campuses though. There had to be instigators behind it, fueling the fire."

"Of course there was. They knew if they could push the right people hard enough, the bullets were going to start flying. It was like waking a sleeping giant. All those folks that normally would have just ignored it and tried to go on about their business finally didn't have a choice anymore, not when it got so that they couldn't *do* business. The whole economy began to collapse when it got to where people couldn't go to work. Stuff started disappearing off the shelves and the faster it went, the crazier the mobs got. They were burning entire cities and nobody could stop them. Restricting travel and communications was the best attempt the feds could make and it might have done some good, but it hurt everyone, not just the troublemakers. I don't have to tell you, son. You've been dealing with it in Europe."

"Yeah all that stuff and more, on top of the endless attacks by jihadists bent on taking the world back to the Middle Ages."

"There's been plenty of that here too; all kinds of mayhem carried out by terrorists taking advantage of the confusion, fear and disruption created by the anarchists. They were feeding off of each other, keeping law enforcement spread so thin they couldn't possibly respond to all of it. Who knows the full extent of it? I haven't heard anything outside the local area since the hurricane hit. Now isn't that something, getting clobbered by a major hurricane on top of all that other crap? I don't think this part of Florida will recover from it, to be honest with you."

"I agree, and that's why it's time to get out. I came here to find Megan and do just that. I was going to come here anyway, even if I found her at the house in North Palm Beach. I wanted to get you, and Shauna and her new family too if they wanted to go, and get as far away from this mess as possible. I figured you'd have a good boat on the hard here or know where one was, and then we'd get outfitted and set sail. Now it looks like all that has changed with Megan still in Colorado. I can't sail there, so I guess I'm going to have to come up with another plan."

"You could go most of the way to the Rockies in the kayak," Jonathan said. "You'd have to paddle up the coast to the Mississippi River and then turn left at St. Louis. I read about some guys that did a trip like that, following the route of Lewis and Clark. It would probably take you a freakin' year to do it though."

"Way longer than I have, that's for sure."

"The boy's got a point though," Bart said. "Just because you can't *sail* to Colorado, that don't mean you can't go a good part of the way by boat. If you could get across the Gulf to Louisiana and up to Keith's place, that would be a start. Last time I talked to Keith he said they were running a lot a barges up the Atchafalaya from the Gulf. With all the refineries on the Texas coast there was still gas there earlier this summer, and the safest way to move it north to the rest of the country was by river. But if the hurricane hit hard up there, things may have changed."

"You haven't talked to him since the storm, have you? From what I understood from the fellow we chatted with by VHF in Florida bay, the hurricane apparently went straight across the Gulf and made landfall in Louisiana. You can bet that stuff got messed up in Keith's AO if it did. He said they'd sailed from Bay St. Louis, and that the entire region was pretty torn up."

"No, it was definitely before the hurricane hit and took out the repeater towers down here. I'm sure he's got his hands full then, if he's dealing with hurricane aftermath. It was bad enough before. He said his department was helping out with the riots in Baton Rogue, and when they weren't over there, they were working the Atchafalaya. Just to tell you how crazy things have been, they had people trying to take out the I-10 Bridge that crosses the swamp there; that and power lines and pipelines too! That's how he knew what was going on with the barge traffic. They were trying to keep the fuel shipments low key because they knew damned well those riverboats would be prime targets if anyone knew they were full of fuel. Anyway, it's something to think about, since it's kind of on your way, no matter how you might try to get to Boulder."

"Power line and pipeline sabotage? No shit? I thought it was the government taking out the grid in certain cities to try and quell the riots."

"They did start doing that, but the anarchists were determined to turn off the lights way before that. Turns out they got what they wanted without even trying. Doesn't make a damned bit of sense does it?"

"Not unless both sides were deliberately trying to make it hard on everybody else—everybody that didn't want any part of this nonsense," Eric said.

"Well, it's hard not to be involved now, no matter who you are. I don't know of anywhere you could go in the Lower 48 and not be affected. Of course you know it's been as bad or worse over in Europe."

"That's exactly why my plan all along was to get a good boat—one that could take us to places nobody gives a damned about fighting over."

Bart made fresh coffee while they discussed this and waited for daylight. He would take Eric and Jonathan to the house afterwards, and he knew Eric would have a lot of questions for Shauna when he got there. Bart could tell the wheels were turning in Eric's mind though, and that he was considering the idea of going to Keith's place like he suggested.

"The boat part of the equation is a no-brainer, the only complication is getting to Colorado first. Going up the Atchafalaya from the Gulf to Keith's place might be a good option to start with though," Eric said. "It's way better than trying to go up the Mississippi, and having to deal with New Orleans and Baton Rogue."

"I doubt you could get through there at all," Bart agreed.

"Where is the Atchafalaya?" Jonathan asked. "I've never even heard of it."

"It's a big river that runs west of the Mississippi; it heads up where the Red River runs into the Mississippi about halfway between Baton Rouge and Natchez. It's connected to the main river by a lock and dam, and some of the traffic coming up and down the Mississippi cuts off there because it runs out to the Gulf down by Morgan City, which is a lot closer to Texas."

"Can you go up a river like that in the kind of sailboat you were talking about getting out of the country in?"

"I don't see why not," Bart said. "It's a navigable river, although I'm not sure about bridge clearances. You might have to drop the masts to get a sailboat under some of them. And you'll need a strong diesel engine to buck the current, I'd imagine."

"We'd need a good diesel regardless," Eric said. "And a mast in a tabernacle would be a huge plus, no matter where we go, especially after we get Megan and leave for good. Knowing how unreliable the wind is in the northern Gulf this time of year, it would be a good idea to have enough fuel range to motor across. What is it, around 450 nautical miles from Fort Myers? Three or four days?"

"Sounds about right. I can think of one vessel I've got here that will fit that description, but we can take a look later. I imagine you'll want to talk to Shauna first though, and get the full story on Megan from her."

Twenty-two

SHAUNA WAS AWAKE BEFORE everyone else as usual, and she was already sitting on the porch sipping coffee when the first hint of daylight began filtering through the palms surrounding the little bungalow. Shauna cherished that hour of alone time each day before Bart returned, as it was the only such time she really had since they'd all been crowded together in his house. But it wasn't Bart she needed time away from so much as it was Daniel. She was glad her husband slept in most mornings, and particularly days like this one, after an argument like the one they'd had last night. Daniel was miserable here, and unable to adapt or develop the patience that was essential to coping with the long days of waiting in limbo. The pace of life here on the river was slower than anything Daniel had ever known. It was driving him crazy, and his inability to deal with it was wearing Shauna out. Bart had completely dismissed Daniel's foolish idea to go back to North Palm Beach by boat, and with no one to help him or agree to go with him it wasn't going to happen. He'd threatened to walk if he had to, and Shauna had told him to go ahead if he thought his house back there was that important. She didn't doubt that he might actually try it at some point, and if he was determined to do so, she wouldn't try to stop him, but she would do her best to talk him out of taking Andrew with him.

As she sat there trying to think of more pleasant things than those arguments while she enjoyed her morning coffee, Shauna was surprised to hear an approaching outboard well before Bart's usual time to return. She left her cup on the rough planking of the picnic table and stepped down off the porch, instinctively reaching to touch the grip of the Glock on her belt. It always reassured her when she did that, even though she hadn't yet had the need to actually draw it from the holster. She wouldn't let down her guard until she knew who was coming, even though the motor sounded like Bart's as it slowed near the mouth of the little creek beside the house.

Shauna crept down the path to the dock, but stayed back among the trees when she heard the boat turn in and reduce to idle speed. When she saw that there were three figures sitting in it instead of just one, she put her hand on the Glock again, but straining to see details through the dim gray light, she recognized Bart in the stern, his hand on the throttle as he steered to the dock. The other two occupants were sitting facing him, so that their backs were to her, but when he came alongside the dock, they both got to their feet and turned her way to ready the lines for tying off. Shauna couldn't believe her eyes. One of Bart's new companions was a scraggly-looking young man she'd never seen before, but the other one was Bart's own son—*Eric Branson!*

Shauna stood there frozen in shock and unable to speak as they secured the boat and stepped onto the dock. When they started up the path to the house, She still said nothing until Bart noticed her standing there among the shadows.

"Shauna! Look what washed up at the boatyard this morning!"

Eric saw her now after hearing Bart address her, so there was no avoiding him any longer.

"Hi Shauna! I got here as soon as I could."

"It's never soon enough though, is it Eric? Did it take a war at home to make you want to come back? Have you got a contract to work here now?"

"You know why I'm back, Shauna! I was hoping Megan would be here with you. I went to your house first, of course, and then I came straight here. But Dad told me she didn't come home for the summer break."

"You went to our house? Is it still there?"

"Yes, it's still there. It didn't get as much damage from the storm as some in the area, but it's been looted. I looked for clues that Megan had been there recently, but didn't really find anything."

"That's because she hasn't been. I've been worried about her all summer, Eric. I wanted to go and try to find her, but it's just impossible now. I've just been hoping she's safe with her friends, and that things aren't as bad in Boulder as they were getting in Denver. We haven't heard any news since the hurricane though, so I have no idea."

"Well if she stayed put, she's probably better off. But wherever she is, I'll find her if it's the last thing I ever do. It's what I came here for and now that I know she was still there the last time any of you talked to her, Colorado is where I'm going next."

"But how?" Shauna asked. "I don't know what your father's told you of the situation, but you know I would have gone if there was a way." Even as she said it though, Shauna knew that impossible wasn't in Eric Branson's vocabulary. He had his faults—many of them—but being intimidated by a tough challenge wasn't one. If anyone could get to Colorado and find Megan, it was Eric, and despite the anger she felt at seeing him here now, she also felt more hope than she'd known since the last time she had spoken with their daughter.

She listened to his brief account of his journey here after being introduced to Jonathan and learning why Eric had brought him along. She also learned that Bart nearly shot both of them before he realized who was in his sights. By then they had made their way up to the porch, and Shauna went inside to put more water on the stove for coffee. As she measured out the grounds to brew another pot, Daniel came down the ladder from the loft.

"Who's here? I heard several people talking out there. It woke me up."

He wasn't going to be thrilled to hear it, but Shauna didn't hesitate to tell him: "Megan's dad. And a friend."

"What? Eric Branson? Are you kidding me? What's that son of a bitch doing here now?"

"Shh! He can probably hear you, Daniel. He's right outside on the porch!"

"Did you tell him Megan wasn't here and that even if she was, she probably wouldn't want to see him?"

"You don't know that she wouldn't. Things are a lot different now. She may have a totally different perspective."

"Do you? It sounds like *you're* happy to see him. I guess he's the good guy now that everybody's walking around with guns all the time. More useful than a guy like me, is that it?"

"Don't be ridiculous, Daniel! Eric is Megan's *father!* I haven't been able to go get her, but if anyone can, *he* can. And he will. He's not going to be hanging around here waiting, so you don't have to worry about that."

Daniel muttered something under his breath that Shauna couldn't hear, but she knew what it was about. Daniel thought he was smarter than Eric and certainly more cultured and successful. He also knew Eric probably felt the same disdain for him because he wasn't a 'warrior' and hadn't done anything particularly brave or dangerous in his life. The two men were opposites, and both of them had their good points and their bad points. Daniel had certainly been easier to live with, at least before, but that was mainly because he liked being at home, which was the one place he *couldn't* be now.

"He went to our house first, before he came here," Shauna said, knowing that would grab Daniel's attention.

"He did? What did he say? Is everything all right over there? Did he say if the power was back on?"

"Why don't you ask him? He can give you all the details first hand and you can ask all the questions you like."

The two men had only met on a couple of occasions, and Shauna knew Daniel was uncomfortable around Eric, but he was here now and there was no avoiding him until he was ready to leave. They were guests in Eric's father's house and that was that. When she led him outside and reintroduced them, along with Jonathan, Daniel's anxiety over his house wiped away any inhibitions he might have had about talking to her ex-husband.

"The hurricane did some wind damage, but nothing major. Like I told Shauna, it was the looters that came afterwards that did the real damage… the front door was kicked in… the cars in the garage were busted up and their tires slashed… everything inside the house torn apart and scattered. It was ransacked pretty thoroughly, man, but it wasn't just yours; it was the whole neighborhood; hell, the whole city."

"Did you see any of the neighbors? Did it look like anyone was at home?"

"No, of course not, it's too dangerous. I saw a man get shot to death right in front of me at the end of your canal. As far as I know, the body is still where it fell, left to rot in the weeds that used to be somebody's lawn. I don't think anyone that lived in that neighborhood stuck around for long, whether they left after the storm or right before it hit like you did. There's no electricity, no running water, no gas, no food and no security. You can't go back there, man. Maybe someday, but not anytime soon."

Shauna saw the change in Daniel's face as the news sunk in. He seemed to believe Eric's matter-of-fact account of what he'd seen, and it was an immense relief to her because maybe at last he would stop talking about it. Maybe he would realize that life as he knew it before had changed forever and it was now time to start making the best of what they had to work with. That kind of change was hard to face, but it was time to accept it and get on with looking forward.

"It looks like all of you have been pretty well set here at my Dad's," Eric said. "I figured I would find you here, and I knew the old man would have this under control. That boatyard is quite the resource when it comes to survival goods."

"As long as you keep the rats out of it," Bart said. "I don't get to sleep at night any more, but that's the cost of doing business, I suppose."

"You've done a helluva job, from what I can see, Dad."

"I'd rather be hauling out boats and running the yard instead of picking off looters, but times have changed, that's for sure. As long as I can get a little rest in the daytime, I'll be all right. I'm gonna need a nap here in a bit, and I imagine you two could use one too after paddling that kayak all night. After that, we'll head back down to the yard and have a look at a vessel I think you're going to like."

Shauna looked from Bart to Eric, but before she could ask her question, Eric answered it.

"What I had in mind all along, Shauna, was to find Megan and get her out of here. It's not safe in Florida, and it's not safe anywhere in the U.S. for the long term. I had planned to come here and outfit a good boat and sail it to someplace that nobody's fighting over. Some place way the hell away from here."

"What makes you think Megan would want to do that? Do you think she'd leave all her friends and everybody else to sail away into the sunset with you? She's hardly seen you in five years, Eric. You don't even know her anymore, and what about me? I'm her mother. Do you think I'd be happy about you taking her away to where I might never see her again?"

"What's the alternative, Shauna? Do you think she'd be safe here in Florida in this situation? You've been okay out here with my dad, but only because it's off the beaten path and hard to find. It won't stay that way indefinitely, and he can't keep people from raiding that boatyard for long. Even good people turn to desperate measures when they have no other alternative. I've seen it too many times, and I can tell you it's a *fact.* And I wasn't planning on just grabbing Megan and leaving. I want my dad to come along, and I was going to ask you and Daniel and Andrew to come as well."

"To go where?" Daniel asked. "How do you know anyplace else is any safer than here? The United States is not going to fall apart because of a bunch of anarchists and terrorists. They're going to get this under control and things will be better here than they were before."

"That would be nice, Daniel, but you know, I've been dealing with this in several countries in Europe for half a decade. Even before it started here, our military was spread thin fighting this kind of crap all over the world. There aren't enough resources left at home to handle something like this if it's as big as I think it is."

"Well, why haven't you been here doing your part? I thought that's what you did for a living?"

Eric ignored the question, but Shauna knew Daniel was going to go too far if she didn't intervene. She got her chance to change the subject when Andrew woke up and came down to see what was going on after hearing all the loud talking. Andrew had met his stepsister's father once before and knew Eric was a soldier of some sort. When he saw him and Jonathan standing there with the M4s slung at their sides, he started in on questions that would have kept them busy all morning. Bart managed to put him on hold so the three men could get a nap though, by promising Andrew they'd take him with them when they went back to the boatyard that afternoon.

When they all finally left in Bart's skiff around 3pm that afternoon, Shauna and Daniel had the house to themselves for the first time since they'd been there. With the loft wide open to the lower level and the rest of the house, they'd not had a moment of privacy in all that time. Shauna knew Daniel wasn't happy about Eric showing up there, and she understood why he felt that way. But after Eric had taken her aside before they left and told her what he and Bart had discussed about sailing to Louisiana, Shauna already knew that she that wanted to go too. Megan wasn't coming back to south Florida on her own, and if Eric had a viable plan to reach her, then Shauna wanted to do her part to help. She had to get Daniel on board with it too, even though she already knew he wasn't going to like it. The first step in making him more agreeable was to reassure him that Eric wasn't a threat. He needed to know he was still her man, even though he hadn't been acting like much of one lately. She took his hand and led him to the foot of the steps that went up to the loft.

"Come on, Daniel, let's go upstairs. They won't be back for three or four hours. Let's spend some time in the moment and forget about our worries. It's been way too long."

Twenty-three

ERIC COULDN'T WAIT TO see the vessel Bart wanted to show him that afternoon. He was full of anticipation and ready to go, even though he'd only slept a few hours. Seeing Shauna again reminded him even more of why he was here, and he intended to waste no time putting together a new plan to reach Megan. The first part of that plan was deciding on a boat. Most of the vessels dry-docked in his father's yard were far from suitable for what he had in mind—either because they were too fuel thirsty, too dependent upon technology, or drew too much water to enter shallow rivers and coves. All of them of course, belonged to someone else, and none of the owners could be reached to inquire as to whether or not they wanted to sell. Eric had told Bart about the gold he was carrying, but it would do little good towards paying for a vessel if there was no one with whom to negotiate a price.

"I've been shooting folks to keep them from stealing things off of those boats, but I've been knowing all along I couldn't hold them off forever. I thought about Keith and Lynn up there in Cajun country and wondered about trying to go to their place, but I knew I couldn't do it on my own." Bart glanced back at Jonathan and Andrew, to make sure Andrew couldn't hear him as he continued on in a whisper. "That Daniel's about worthless when it comes to doing anything with his hands, and the boy's too young to be much help, even if they would have agreed to go with me. Now that you're here, I know Shauna's gonna want to go, at least as far as Keith's, just so she'll be that much closer to Megan."

"I hope so. She's got no business staying here, especially not if you're going."

"Well, you know I hate to give up my place here, and I wasn't planning on letting it go until they killed me for it, but the way things are looking, that's probably just a matter of time. Whether I die here or leave first, these boats are all gonna be stripped and the better ones will probably be taken if the fools can figure out how to launch them. I hate to make off with somebody's boat myself, but I reckon if the owners aren't here to get them by now, they probably never will be. I know for sure that the folks that own the one I've got in mind won't be able to get here. There ain't no way in hell."

"Why not? Where are they?"

"Toronto. They've been keeping their boat down here since before I bought the yard. They're retired now, of course and they come down every year after Thanksgiving and go to the Bahamas or Cuba for two or three months, then they come back up the river and haul out again and go home."

"Sounds like a nice way to escape the Canadian winter."

"Yep, but they're several years older than I am; probably both pushing seventy-five if I had to guess. That's why I know they're not gonna be showing up to get their boat with things the way they are. They were already slowing down before all this happened and said they might skip it this coming winter anyway. For their sake, I hope they don't try. First off, they'd have to get across the border and then somehow cross the whole country to get here. It ain't gonna happen, if you ask me, so their boat's gonna stay sitting where she is like all the rest of them. Another thing is that they don't have any children, so they were probably going to leave it to charity anyway when they died, if they didn't sell it first, and I don't think the old man could have brought himself to do that. He'd probably rather see you take it to sea than think about that, and for what you want to do, it's the best vessel I've got in the yard. She's well-kept and well-equipped too, and it won't take more than a few days to recommission her."

Eric followed Bart through the rows of fiberglass sailboats and gleaming motor yachts to the back of the boatyard, where several larger sailing vessels were blocked up with their sterns to the chain-link fence at the back perimeter. All of the boats in this row were serious cruisers, and like the one Bart wanted to show him, were owned by folks who lived in other places and mainly sailed them in the winter months. When they came to the end of the row, Eric saw a hard-chined metal hull with a shallow full keel, everything above the waterline hidden by a full-length canvas cover. Two massive wooden spars were lying on sawhorses alongside the hull, and Eric noted the heavy, oversized standing rigging and turnbuckles.

"Steel hull?" he asked.

"Nope, all aluminum; custom-built. She's a Tom Colvin design, built right here on the river in 1987 I believe."

"The masts look like they're both about the same length. Schooner rigged?"

"Yep, lots of sail options for all kinds of weather. She's got a rebuilt 50-horsepower Perkins diesel in her too. Just with her onboard tankage, she's got a 400-mile range under power. With all the Jerry cans we can scrounge up from around the yard, you could load her down with enough for a few hundred more. Hey Andrew! Jonathan! Give us a hand with this cover. Let's get it off so we can have a good look at her."

When the cover came off and Eric stood back to get a look at the schooner's lines, he was impressed. The best thing of all was that she looked like a working vessel and not a yacht. Above the waterline, the topsides and cabin trunks were painted flat gray, almost the same shade favored by the Navy. Eric walked around to the stern and read the name on her transom: *Tropicbird.* It seemed fitting for a Canadian sailing vessel seeking escape to the warm waters of the islands. Bart got a ladder from under the jack stands and leaned it up against the starboard rail.

"Come on aboard, and see what you think."

Eric already knew he was going to like what he saw. The helm was located in the well-protected cockpit between the main cabin and a smaller, separate aft cabin. It was a good layout for a large crew, which is what they would have if everyone at Bart's house agreed to go. Like the topsides, the decks and deck-fittings were all business and no-nonsense. Cleats, stanchions and pulpits were welded in place, and other than the cockpit sole, which was planked with teak; the decks were painted with off-white nonskid. What really set her apart from the mass-produced sailing yachts more commonly seen was the fact that there were tabernacles for the two masts. Eric assumed the spars had been removed for long-term storage, but with this stepping arrangement, once they were reinstalled they could be raised and lowered from on deck without the help of machinery other than the onboard winches. It was a great feature and one they would need if they had to pass under low, fixed bridges. Even drawbridges built to open for vessel traffic would be inoperable now, so having the means to drop the masts was a huge plus.

"It looks like she was designed for serious voyaging," Eric said, his appraisal complete even before he looked below decks.

"Anywhere you want to go, son; around the world if need be. This one hasn't done it, but some of her sister ships have circumnavigated for sure."

"It wouldn't make sense to go around; you'd just end up back here, wouldn't you?" Jonathan asked as he and Andrew followed the two older men forward to check out the windlass and bowsprit.

"That's right," Eric laughed. "Exactly *halfway* would be much better. Then, we'd be as far away from here as possible."

"Man, that sounds like an adventure! I'll bet the fishing is great at some of those islands out there. That would be awesome!"

"I've been deep sea fishing in the Gulf Stream," Andrew said. "My dad's company used to charter boats like that one to take us out." Andrew pointed at one of the sport fishing yachts blocked up in the yard. "We had our own boat too and we used to go out pretty far when the weather was good."

"Have you ever sailed, Andrew?" Eric asked.

"No sir. My dad said sailboats are too slow and he didn't have enough time off work to go that slow. He said life was too short for that."

"Maybe before," Eric laughed. "Not now though."

"Sailing's pretty cool, actually," Jonathan said. "I'd never sailed either until I hooked up with Eric. I'll bet a real boat like this is even more badass—especially crossing the whole ocean. That would be a trip!"

Bart opened up the two cabins and they all went below to explore the accommodations. Like everything on deck, the interior was sensible and well thought out, rather than showy. All of the interior woodwork was dark mahogany, hand-rubbed with an oil finish. There was a U-shaped galley with a four-burner propane stove and oven, and a deep stainless steel sink with foot pumps for both fresh and salt water. Eric made a mental note as he counted the bunks. There were enough to make it work, even with an extra crewmember. Getting everyone to Louisiana was the only consideration for now. After he found Megan, there would be other decisions to make about what to do next and who would go with him. At this point that was so far beyond the present it didn't figure into Eric's calculations at all. The only thing about that future he could think of now was whether this was the boat that would make it a reality, and after seeing it inside and out, he was certain that it was.

"What needs doing before she can be launched?" Eric asked Bart.

"Mostly just the usual maintenance; slap on a fresh coat of bottom paint, repack the stuffing box and change out the zincs, change the engine oil and put a couple of coats of vanish on the spars. That's off the top of my head. We'll check everything though. If it's just you and me working, it might take four or five days. If your buddy here wants to help and knows how to work, that might speed it up."

"I don't mind working," Jonathan said.

"When I met him, he was camping in the mangroves over near Jupiter Inlet. He'd been stranded there since somebody stole his boat. I told him if he wanted to help me sail over here that we might be able to find him another skiff of some kind. Jonathan's quite the fisherman. All he needs is a boat and he's set."

"Until somebody comes along and steals that one too," Bart said. "Or worse."

"It's a dangerous world," Eric agreed.

"Hell, you can have *my* skiff after we leave," Bart told Jonathan. "I won't have use for it. You can stay at the house too, for that matter. If we all go, it's just gonna be left for the looters to clean out."

"I don't imagine I can hold them off on my own," Jonathan said. "Especially with just a .357 Magnum. I'll probably end up living in the woods again, where I won't attract any attention."

"Or you could just go with us," Eric said. "We could use another crewmember that knows how to sail. And when we get to Louisiana, I think you'll find that there's some damned fine fishing in the Atchafalaya," Eric grinned. He saw the kid's jaw drop at the offer. Clearly Jonathan had never expected an opportunity like this.

"Really? You'd take me with you?"

"If you'll do your part, and if you understand the risks. I have no idea what we'll run into up there, or even trying to get out of here. You already saw the blockade at Fort Myers, and you saw what happened off Biscayne Bay. You might be a lot safer staying here at my dad's place, but then again, you might not. It's up to you, bud."

"Man, I don't even have to think about it; I'm in! Just tell me what to do, and I'll get to work! I can paint or whatever, I really don't mind! It would be cool to see someplace new for a change, even if it's worse than here. I'm not afraid of the risks. I could die here any day, like you said."

"Good deal, welcome aboard then! I imagine we'll get started on the work in the morning, right Dad?"

"Yeah, but we still need to keep watch over the yard at night, especially now. It would be just our luck that somebody would come along and do something to mess up the *Tropicbird* if we don't."

"I'll do it, and give you a break," Eric said. "Jonathan will stay too and swap shifts with me, won't you Jonathan?"

"You bet! But how are we going to get a big boat like this out to the Gulf with that blockade down there at the mouth of the river? We can't sneak this one through the mangroves, that's for sure."

"That's a good question, but one we'll worry about later. First we have to get it ready and get it back in the water. A boat on the hard is no boat at all, right Dad?"

"That's right. But it is a good question. I don't know if the waterway is open going east or not, but that would sure be a long way out of the way. Maybe it's possible to negotiate with whoever's in charge of that blockade. It sounds to me like it's more about keeping vessels from entering the river than it is to keep someone from leaving."

"We'll figure it out. Why don't you take Andrew and go on back home and get some rest? Come get us at first light and we'll drink some coffee and have breakfast with all of you at the house. I want to have another talk with Shauna and see if she's on board or not, and then we can get back here and get started."

When Bart and Andrew motored away in the skiff, Eric and Jonathan went in the yard office where Eric had stowed most of his gear from the kayak. Then, the two of them made a simple meal from the rations they'd lived on while sailing around Florida.

"Dude, I sure hope they all agree to go with us. What are you going to do if your ex-wife and her husband say they won't do it? We're going anyway, right?"

"Of course we are. They'd be foolish to stay here alone though. I know that's what he wants to do, but Shauna's smarter than that. Without my dad here to help them, they'd be in trouble soon. And I know Dad wants to go, because my brother's up there, and he's always been closer to him than me anyway."

"That Daniel dude seems like a pain in the ass. I don't know what your ex sees in him anyway. She's pretty fine, man. Why in the hell did you let *her* go? If I had a woman like that at home, I wouldn't ever leave the house!"

"I don't know. I'm just stupid, I guess. What can I say?"

Twenty-four

THEIR NIGHT WATCH AT the boatyard turned out to be uneventful, and Eric was anxious to get back to the house and talk to Shauna when he heard his father's outboard approaching at the crack of dawn. He hoped he could get a few minutes alone with her, away from Daniel, because he wanted her undivided attention so he could get his answers and get back to the yard to get started working on the boat. When Bart pulled into the slipway to pick them up though, Eric had his doubts.

"Everybody's up and Shauna and Daniel are already making breakfast. Did you have any trouble out here last night? I didn't hear any rifle shots."

"Didn't see a thing," Eric said. "Did you tell Shauna about the boat? Did you tell her we're going to get started on it today."

"Yep. She asked me a lot of questions, but she really wants to talk to you some more. Said to tell you there's some things about Megan you don't know about."

"I image there are. I haven't seen her much since Shauna found her a stepdad. I was hoping he was still asleep. How am I supposed to talk to her now without him getting in the middle of everything? He's going to say something that'll piss me off, and that'll be that."

"Maybe, but he seems to be in a better mood. He was in a better mood when I got back there yesterday evening. Maybe they talked it over, who knows?"

"Or maybe he just got laid while everyone was out of the house for a while," Eric said, eliciting a chuckle from Jonathan. Eric thought he didn't care what Shauna was doing, but he knew deep inside that he still did in a way. Seeing her again yesterday brought back a lot of memories, both good and bad. She'd tried hard to make it work—she'd begged him to find another occupation and stay here in Florida with her and their child. He'd done his best at the time, but in the end, he'd left one time too many and that was that. He tried not to think about her and what might have been most of the time, and when he came here his only objective was finding Megan. Shauna wanted the same thing, but she didn't want him, and Eric had to remind himself of that until it sunk in. Anything else was wishful thinking. Eric got his time alone with her to talk though. After they'd all eaten breakfast, Daniel stayed in the house with Andrew while Shauna walked with Eric down to the dock.

"He's sure in a better mood today," Eric said.

"He's been under a lot of stress, Eric. I know it's hard for you to understand, but his whole world has been turned upside down. He hasn't had the kinds of experiences you have. Living off the grid like this is all new to him. He's lost everything."

"No he hasn't. He's got you, and he's got his son. I'd say he's a lot better off than most people these days."

"We didn't come here to talk about him though, did we?"

"No, but I need to know if you're going with us, and I imagine that depends on whether he's going or not."

"He thinks it's insane. He doesn't want to think about it right now. He'll come around, I've just got to ease him into the idea, just like with the idea of coming here."

"Well, don't go too easy. We'll be launching the boat in three or four days. Maybe faster if you two would help us. Whether you do or not, I've got to get Jonathan and Bart and get back down there before the morning is gone. What exactly is it that you want to tell me about Megan? Is there something you know that you haven't told her grandfather? Do you know something else about where she is?"

"No, I have some ideas but I don't know for sure."

"What ideas? That she may be somewhere besides Colorado?"

"No, at least I don't think so, just ideas about the people she might be associated with. I hope I'm wrong, but I'm worried that she might have put herself in more danger than she would be in otherwise."

"What do you mean, 'put herself' in it? Why would she do something like that? She's smarter than that."

"She's smart, but she's also stubborn, Eric. I'm afraid there's a whole lot about our daughter that you don't know. You haven't been around her much at all since she was in her early teens. She's not the little girl you remember."

"She seemed pretty normal last time I saw her. She was eighteen then. What's changed since?"

"She's pretty good at hiding a lot of things, Eric. She wouldn't get in a confrontational conversation with you, because she'd be afraid to. She'd rather just pretend than bring it up."

"A conversation about what? I know she's not crazy about what I do for a living, but she's old enough to understand the necessity of it by now, right?"

"She's old enough, Eric, but that doesn't mean she does, and neither do the friends she hangs out with."

"So? That's normal right? College kids her age are all about peace and love and music. I know she decided she didn't like guns, even though she used to love shooting back when we did it. I can see her being embarrassed to tell all her new friends out there on campus that her dad is a contractor who makes his living killing terrorists, when their professors probably tell them the terror threat isn't even real. She's bound to have gotten a dose of reality by now though—all of them have. Hopefully she's staying put and keeping a low profile since things got ugly."

"I wish I could believe that, Eric, but I don't know. The last time she was home she seemed more distant than ever. I'm worried that she got caught up in something bigger than she thought it was going to be, especially since I haven't heard from her since the real bad stuff started happening. You know there were major riots in Denver, and that's not far at all from Boulder. It was one of the first cities they cut the power to, and there were a lot of people shot. I just hope she wasn't caught up in all that."

"Megan? She's got better sense than to get in the middle of a riot, Shauna. She would know to go the other way if she saw something like that happening."

"She would have at one time, Eric, but now I'm not so sure. You don't know how much influence some of her friends might have had on her. I'm worried that she might have been right in the middle of it!"

"You mean with the anarchists? Why in the hell would Megan get involved with people like that?"

"I don't know, why does anyone? Because of the stuff they hear repeated so much by the media that they start to believe it, I guess. A lot of things have been changing here for years, Eric. I don't have to tell you that. You've been dealing with it in Europe where it's been worse for a whole lot longer. People have never been so divided, and never been so angry. And the longer it went on, the more things happened to fuel that anger and divisiveness. People have been taking sides, and it's not always the side you'd think they'd take."

"So now you're telling me you think our daughter has been running with the people trying to overthrow the government? I thought she was against violence? She might disagree with a lot of policies, and I do too, but she wouldn't try to hurt anyone, would she?"

"Not directly, no. But she could certainly *be* hurt just by her associations. She might even be locked up for all I know. They've got detainment centers all over the country where they're holding dissidents. There's no telling how many innocents like her that could be in those places simply because they were in the wrong place at the wrong time."

"Well I guess I really screwed up royally as a father then, didn't I? Maybe if I'd been here to set an example, she wouldn't have gone off on a tangent like that."

"Maybe, or maybe not. I don't know if she would have listened to you if you had been here or not. I remember how it was to be a teenager, and you probably do too. You think you know it all, and that everyone else is an idiot. But none of that matters now anyway, because you can't change the past, Eric, and I can't either. All we can do is try and find her wherever she is and get her out. I've been going crazy with worry all summer, but there just wasn't anything I could do alone. I couldn't go out there looking for her and Daniel couldn't help me, especial not with Andrew as his first responsibility. But when I first saw you here yesterday, I suddenly had hope again. I know if anyone can go and get our daughter back, it's you, Eric."

"What I really should have done was put the two of you on a boat like *Tropicbird* fifteen years ago and gotten us the hell out of here. We should have sailed to the islands somewhere and raised Megan away from all this screwed up crap in the U.S. I knew this was coming, it was inevitable and just a matter of time. But the Navy owned me back then, and I let them change me into someone I don't even recognize anymore. I lost myself and I lost you and Megan in the process. I'm sorry, Shauna."

He opened his arms and Shauna fell into his embrace, the tears running down her face and onto his shoulder as he held her tightly. "I'm going to find our little girl, Shauna, and I'll bring her back. We'll get across the Gulf first and regroup at Keith's place, and then I'll be on my way. I know I've let you down before, but you've just got to trust me on this one. Nothing matters more to me."

"I want to believe you, Eric. I really do, but you know what you've put us through. It's hard to have that faith anymore."

The words stung because Eric knew his ex-wife was right. He'd let a lot of people down, but those days were over. He had a single-minded focus now, and it was no longer about him or a sense of duty to strangers. Once his father and Shauna and her family were all safely at Keith and Lynn's place, he would no longer have to worry about any of them. It would all be about Megan. Getting them there was no small undertaking, but at least he had the means to accomplish it in the form of a seaworthy schooner waiting in Bart's boatyard. The voyage was just a small step in the journey he was undertaking though, and south Louisiana was still a long way from Boulder in a world where using roads was no longer an option. Bart's idea of working his way upriver on one of the fuel barges seemed as reasonable as any, and Eric would figure it out when he got there. The only thing he knew for sure was that all of this was going to take time, and time was something Megan may not have. Maybes and what ifs were just speculation though. Eric had work to do and he was ready to get started. He relaxed his embrace and kissed Shauna's tear-streaked cheek as he pulled away, stepping into the skiff to start the outboard as she walked back to the house to tell Bart and Jonathan it was time to go to work.

About the Author

SCOTT B. WILLIAMS HAS been writing about his adventures for more than twenty-five years. His published work includes dozens of magazine articles and twelve books, with more projects currently underway. His interest in backpacking, sea kayaking and sailing small boats to remote places led him to pursue the wilderness survival skills that he has written about in his popular survival nonfiction books such as *Bug Out: The Complete Plan for Escaping a Catastrophic Disaster Before It's Too Late*. He has also authored travel narratives such as *On Island Time: Kayaking the Caribbean*, an account of his two-year solo kayaking journey through the islands. With the release of *The Pulse* in 2012, Scott moved into writing fiction and has written several more novels with many more in the works. To learn more about his upcoming books or to contact Scott, visit his website: www.scottbwilliams.com

Made in the USA
Middletown, DE
17 January 2019